The
Turncoat
Thrush

The wild-eyed young man staggered into Del Floria's shop, gasping for breath.

"Let me in!" he pleaded to Del Floria. "Let me into U.N.C.L.E. headquarters! THRUSH is after me; they'll kill me if you don't let me inside!"

Del Floria surreptitiously pressed a button under the counter.

"I was a member of THRUSH," gasped the fugitive, "until I found out the truth about them. I can tell U.N.C.L.E. everything!"

Suddenly the door burst open and two men pushed their way through. The man in the lead pulled a pistol from his pocket; the other man had a blackjack in his hand.

Silently and deliberately, they closed in on the terrified young man.

U.N.C.L.E.

This is the twelfth in Ace Books' series of exciting MAN FROM U.N.C.L.E. novels. For information on earlier books, see page 160.

THE MAN FROM U.N.C.L.E.

NUMBER 12

The Mind-Twisters Affair

Thomas Stratton

Ace Books Inc.
1120 Avenue of the Americas
New York, N.Y. 10036

THE MIND-TWISTERS AFFAIR

AUTHOR'S DEDICATION:
To Jean and Dean Grennell.

THE MIND-TWISTERS AFFAIR

CROSSTOWN TRAFFIC in mid-Manhattan was stalled, the normal state of affairs for the daylight hours. The large black sedan inched its way forward through the sweltering afternoon heat, working resolutely toward the East River. The driver, his jacket off and tie at half mast, was sweating and muttering under his breath. The second man in the front seat was swiveled around, his eyes on the younger man sitting directly behind the driver. The younger man sat stiffly, with a look of quiet desperation in his eyes. He was being watched intently by the other back-seat passenger, who sat with his jacket draped across his lap, his right hand hidden beneath the jacket.

A horn blasted from a few yards away, and the driver jumped slightly and glanced around. Another horn sounded; the driver swore but didn't bother to look for the source of the noise. He stared belligerently ahead while voicing his opinion of all New York drivers except himself.

Suddenly there was a crash and the car lurched forward. The four men were jerked backward into the seat cushions, then tossed forward as the car was stopped suddenly by the rear end of the sports car in front of it. Three of the men turned automatically and angrily toward the rear. The younger man in the back seat lunged for the door. Before any of the others could turn back, he was out of the car and ducking through the stalled traffic.

"Get him!" the driver ordered, and the other two men leaped out of the car. More horns blared as traffic tried to move forward another few feet with three pedestrians ducking through it. The driver pulled an object resembling a cigarette box out of his jacket pocket and began speaking into it.

The younger man snaked his way between the cars and shoved through the crowds on the sidewalk. An alley opened in front of him and he plunged into it and ran. He knew without turning that two of his recent captors would be pursuing him. He had just reached the intersecting alley when the pursuers burst through the crowd and entered the alley. He raced around the corner before they could fire, plunged the length of the alley, and disappeared into the crowd. Now he had a chance; even the vast resources of his pursuers would be taxed to locate a single man in downtown Manhattan when that man didn't want to be located. He didn't know the exact location of the place for which he was heading, but it couldn't be far. The fact that an opportunity had come when it did, after days of patient waiting, was surely a good omen.

He moved rapidly through the crowd; he had a chance, but he was the last person to underestimate the pursuit. There was a commotion in the crowd behind him as someone tried to force his way through the press. He speeded up, noticed that traffic was stalled again, and cut across the street, going through another alley on the opposite side. There was a policeman at the next corner. He thought momentarily of seeking police aid, but discarded the idea. He'd be shot down while the police were still trying to decide whether or not to believe his story. There was only one group which could help him—if he could locate it in time.

Glancing back, he saw no sign of pursuit. His brief elation was stilled by the thought of the number of reinforcements his hunters could pour into the area. He hurried on, winded now and beginning to breathe heavily.

Minutes later, he rounded a final corner and spotted the sign he had been looking for. "Del Floria—Cleaners" it read. He raced for it and staggered as he entered, gasping for breath. His recent enforced inactivity was beginning to tell on him. Del Floria, a little man in his fifties, looked up from behind the shop counter at the sudden intrusion.

The fugitive lurched across the floor to the counter. Between gasps for breath, he spoke. "Let me in! I can help you! Let me in before they catch me!"

Del Floria looked puzzled but unperturbed, as if he was used to strange men coming into his shop and shouting at him. "Let you in? As far as I can see, you are in."

"No, no! Into U.N.C.L.E. headquarters. You have to trust me. Thrush is after me; they know I'll come here and they can't be far behind. They'll kill me if you don't let me inside!"

"I told you . . ." Del Floria began again, this time surreptitiously pressing a button recessed under the counter.

"You don't understand," the man rushed on, beginning to regain his breath. "I was a member of Thrush, until I found out the truth about them. I can tell U.N.C.L.E. all sorts of things."

"The truth about Thrush?"

"They're a bunch of international gangsters!" A look of fanaticism came across the man's face. "They're evil; they must be destroyed! I'll do anything to help U.N.-C.L.E. against them. I did their terrible work for ten years! I must get in! I must have a chance to make up for those years!"

Del Floria preserved his air of incomprehension while pushing the button a second time. Where was that security detail? The man was close to sobbing now, pounding his fist on the counter.

Suddenly the door burst open again. This time two men in their shirtsleeves pushed their way through, the man in the lead pulling a pistol from his pocket as he entered. The man at the counter whirled around, terrified. He screamed at the sight of the two men, then dashed blindly toward the rear of the shop.

"It's somewhere here, it has to be!" he cried, pounding at the walls around the dressing booths.

The man with the gun stood just inside the doorway, watching both Del Floria and the fugitive. The second man, a huge individual, approached the fugitive, a black-jack gripped in one beefy hand.

As the pursuer approached, the fugitive turned from his futile pounding of the walls and swung a fist at his opponent. The man with the blackjack avoided the blow and grabbed the smaller man's wrist. With a quick twist, the fugitive broke free and darted for the doorway. With a speed amazing in so large a man, the pursuer was on him. The blackjack swung once, and the victim crumpled to the shop floor.

Quickly and efficiently, the two men carried the unconscious form from the shop, the leader eyeing Del Floria all the time. However, neither man made a move toward the shop's proprietor, and as they reached the street, the large man even reached back to carefully close the shop door.

A moment later, when the security detail came hurriedly out of the dressing booth which served as an entrance to U.N.C.L.E. headquarters, the shop was peaceful.

CONTENTS

Section I : "Put On His Most Cynical Sneer"

Chapter 1 : "Our Image Appears To Have Become Tarnished" 13

2 : "The Hardest Part Is Finding A Rose With Hips" 25

3 : "What's Your Excuse For Starting This Riot?" 33

4 : "Habit, Nothing But Habit" 42

Section II : "Harass The Foe From The Rear"

5 : "How Does One Lose A Helicopter?" 51

6 : "What Is All This Stuff Under Here?" 59

7 : "The Thing To Do Is Work Out A New Questionnaire" 66

8 : "A Powerful Figure Of Evil Indeed" 77

Section III : "You're Anxious To End Your Career?"

9 : "If I Didn't Know Better, I'd Say This Was A Chain" 90

10 : "You're Developing A Very Creditable Mean Streak" 97

11 : "Who Ever Heard Of A Flying Saucer With A Parachute?" 106

Section IV : "Likewise, Give The Victor A Cheer"

12 : "I Don't Care If They Flapped Their Wings And Flew" 117

13 : "How Does 'Whateley For President' Strike You?" 124

14 : "This Isn't Exactly What I Had In Mind" 131

15 : "Clumsiness Pays Off Again" 139

16 : "It's A Little Late To Call Mr. Waverly" 147

Chapter 1

"Our Image Appears To Have Become Tarnished"

NAPOLEON SOLO and Illya Kuryakin walked respectfully into the office. Alexander Waverly stood at the window, puffing on his pipe and staring contemplatively at the U.N. building a few blocks away. An elderly gnome of a man with an Einstein-style bush of gray hair paced nervously behind Waverly and looked up suddenly as Illya closed the office door.

"Dr. Morthley," Napoleon said, holding out his hand. "It's nice to see you again. How are you coming with your invisibility device?"

Dr. Morthley's welcoming grin faded. "Terrible," he replied. "I haven't been able to make any progress at all since you got me away from Thrush last spring."

Napoleon shook his head sympathetically. "Getting kidnapped by Thrush and spirited away to Central America in an invisible dirigible can be an unsettling experience. Perhaps it's simply taken you a while to recover from the shock."

"Yes," Illya agreed. "I'm sure you'll find a way to make the device practical."

"My feelings precisely, gentlemen," Waverly said, moving toward his large, circular desk. "Dr. Morthley has indicated the need for a fresh viewpoint, which is why I've called you here."

Napoleon raised an eyebrow. "I'm afraid that science was never my strongest subject, sir," he said, looking questioningly at Illya.

"And invisibility wasn't mine," Illya added.

"No, no, gentlemen; you misunderstand. The man we want is Dr. Richard Armden. Unfortunately, we seem to be having some difficulty in acquiring his services."

"Armden?" Illya looked thoughtful. "I seem to have heard that name before."

Waverly smiled as he replaced his pipe in its rack. "Correct, Mr. Kuryakin. Dr. Armden has worked with us before, though always in a minor capacity. That is the fact which makes our present predicament particularly puzzling."

The two agents watched Waverly patiently as he motioned them to sit down. He would explain things in his own time and way, and further questions would simply delay him in his selection of another pipe from the well-stocked rack in front of him. Waverly was one of the few individuals who chain-smoked pipes. After a minute of tamping and puffing, during which time Dr. Morthley resumed his pacing, the U.N.C.L.E. Director resumed.

"You are both familiar with Dr. Morthley's device, and the fact that there are certain problems still to be, ah, conquered, before it can be made practical for our use. Approximately a month ago, Dr. Morthley felt that he could benefit from a fresh viewpoint on the problem. He suggested that we contact a former colleague of his, Dr. Armden, from Indiana. Since Dr. Armden had worked with us previously, this struck me as a splendid idea."

Dr. Morthley stopped pacing and flopped down in a

chair. "I don't understand it," he said querulously. "I always considered Richard to be a brilliant man, and he was one of my closest friends when we were both on the Purdue faculty. I simply don't understand his reaction to my phone call, and now this letter . . ."

"Letter, sir?" Napoleon asked, looking inquiringly at both Morthley and Waverly.

Dr. Morthley pulled a crumpled envelope from the pocket of his equally crumpled coat and handed it to Napoleon. Waverly held up a hand and resumed his interrupted lecture.

"Before you read the letter, gentlemen, let me give you the proper background. You see, when we wrote to Dr. Armden, he ignored us completely. We wrote two letters and sent a telegram, with no reply to any of them."

"That just wasn't like Richard," Dr. Morthley broke in, getting to his feet and beginning to pace again. "I became concerned and telephoned him. His wife answered the phone, and at first he refused to speak to me. It sounded as if she had to plead with him before he came to the phone. And when he did . . ." Morthly broke off, shaking his head sadly. After a short pause, he continued. "I'm positive that he's in some sort of trouble. He wouldn't act that way if he wasn't. I've worked with him; he's one of these men who is completely dedicated to his work. I was even a little surprised when he got married, but this! Why, the man never had a political thought in his life!"

Napoleon looked faintly surprised. "I was under the impression that U.N.C.L.E. was above such mundane activity as politics. Disinterested international group, and all that."

"Oh, we are," Mr. Waverly assented. "But our image, at least in the midwest, appears to have become tarnished. What Dr. Morthley started to say was that Dr. Armden refused to help on the grounds that he would never again work for a—I believe the exact words were 'thieving, communistic, war-mongering' organization like U.N.C.L.E."

"Exactly," said Morthley, "and then he heaped abuse on me, just for associating with you! And he hung up on me."

Napoleon reflected that this might be the major source of the scientist's outrage; probably no one else had ever hung up on Willard Morthley since he had achieved his reputation as one of the finest scientific tinkerers since Edison.

"That was last week," Waverly continued. "Then, just yesterday, Dr. Morthley received that letter which you have in your hand, Mr. Solo. It's from Mrs. Armden. She appears quite concerned about her husband's mental state."

Napoleon glanced quickly through the letter and handed it to Illya.

"There's a hysterical tone to parts of it," Napoleon said. "There must be more to it than just his sudden aversion to U.N.C.L.E. and a general irritability. She sounds as if she fears for his sanity."

Waverly nodded and puffed on his pipe. "My opinion precisely, Mr. Solo. That's why I would like you and Mr. Kuryakin to take a look into it first hand. I agree with Dr. Morthley that something unusual must have happened to change Dr. Armden's attitude so rapidly and radically. It was less than a year ago that he last did a small job for us."

Illya looked up suddenly. "Remember that report we got from Security a few months ago? About the man who came into Del Floria's shop, claiming to be a former Thrush who had seen the error of his ways? At the time we accepted it at face value, but the idea of a Thrush agent suddenly changing sides is at least as improbable as what we have here—and the cases seem quite similar."

Waverly nodded. "Exactly. I confess that I cannot conceive of anything that would make a Thrush agent and a respected scientist both change their opinions of humanity in general and U.N.C.L.E. in particular, but it creates intriguing possibilities."

"Just the same, isn't image-making a little out of our line?" Napoleon asked. "Wouldn't this be something for the public relations department in Section 7 to handle?"

"Possibly; however, I'm afraid that Ethel hasn't yet forgiven us for sending her all the way over to the Bronx last week to speak at a Rotary Club luncheon. I don't think she'd react favorably to a request to fly out to Indiana to change the opinion of one scientist."

"Haven't the Directors given her an assistant yet?" Illya inquired. "I thought you promised her one when Kay left to write television scripts."

Waverly concentrated on his pipe for a moment before replying. "You know the budget, Mr. Kuryakin. And we like to think that all our agents help keep our public image spotless."

"Of course, sir," Napoleon agreed instantly, giving Illya a smug look. "You were saying . . . ?"

"You and Mr. Kuryakin will drive out to see Dr. Armden personally. Find out what has made him so violently opposed to us and try to rectify any misconceptions he may have formed since he last worked with us."

"Drive, sir?" Napoleon asked distastefully.

"Correct, Mr. Solo. Dr. Armden lives in Midford, Indiana, a small university town some distance from the nearest airport. In fact, the town has no public transportation. Of course, you could fly in to Fort Wayne and rent a car there, but there is no immediate crisis requiring your attention. You can afford a leisurely drive across country. I understand the leaves are just beginning to turn." Waverly sighed quietly. "You might even regard it as a sort of vacation. I almost wish I could take the time myself. It's very beautiful this time of year."

Napoleon glanced at Illya. Neither seemed thrilled over the prospect of pastoral perfection. "Vacation," he said.

"Quite right, Mr. Solo. As an additional attraction, I have persuaded the other Directors to allow you to drive the special U.N.C.L.E. car."

Napoleon brightened slightly. "I've heard it's quite a car, sir. I've been hoping for a chance to try it out."

"I rather suspected you might. Bear in mind, however, that its devices are intended to be used against Thrush and not for evading traffic officers. And that speeding tickets are not paid for by U.N.C.L.E."

"Of course, sir," Napoleon agreed. "Our public image . . ."

"I don't mean to sound stupid," Illya said, "but I'm afraid I haven't been keeping up to date as Napoleon evidently has. Just what is special about the new car?"

Waverly smiled briefly. "I'm sure Mr. Solo will be more than willing to fill you in on all the details later. A few of the salient points include flame throwers behind the grill, a laser system, rocket launchers in the doors, a device for laying a smoke screen, a bullet-proof shield, a high speed supercharged exhaust, and a braking parachute for emergency stops."

"I hope they have securely locked garages in Indiana," Illya remarked.

"There's no need to be apprehensive, Mr. Kuryakin. A channel in the car's computer has been programmed to respond to a special voice code from your communicators."

"Computer, sir?" Illya looked skeptical.

"Oh, didn't I mention that? It's something our engineering department developed. It's really quite versatile; a step beyond the miniature integrated circuit models most missiles use. There is a direct radio link with our main data and communications center here in New York."

Illya looked impressed at the mention of something more advanced than integrated circuits, but still had a few doubts. "I hope, sir," he said after a moment's reflection, "that such rudimentary devices as seat belts have not been overlooked?"

Midford struck Napoleon as being similar to Mukwanago, the little town in Wisconsin where the search for Thrush's invisible dirigible had begun. Distinguishing between small towns, however, had never been one of Napoleon's strong points; anything much smaller than Chicago struck him as a village. The major distinguishing feature of Midford was Midford University whose enrollment almost equalled the town's native population.

The university was a sprawling affair, made up of several blocks of one- and two-story buildings on the north edge of town. Three-quarters of a mile away, near the southwestern edge of town, was a branch plant of Falco Industries, where Dr. Armden was employed. It turned out he lived only a few blocks from the plant, near the end of a street which dead-ended at an open field a few doors farther on.

Napoleon made a short U-turn at the end of the street and pulled up behind a dark green Sprite with a racing stripe running along the hood. As they got out, Napoleon eyed the stripe for a second and glanced at the unmarked gray surface of the U.N.C.L.E. car.

"I suppose using the computer in a rally would be unsporting," he said regretfully.

"Very," Illya agreed as he rang the front door bell.

A few seconds later, the door opened cautiously. A small woman, apparently in her late forties, peered out, squinting against the setting sun.

"What can I do for you?" she inquired.

"I'm Napoleon Solo and this is Illya Kuryakin," Napoleon began, holding out his identity card.

Before he had a chance to say more, the woman darted out onto the porch, closing the door softly behind her. "From U.N.C.L.E.?" she asked. "You're the ones who've been writing to Richard?"

"Mrs. Armden?" Illya inquired. Receiving a nod, he continued. "It was actually our superior, Mr. Waverly, who wrote your husband; he and Dr. Morthley. But we represent U.N.C.L.E. and . . ."

"I'm very glad to meet you," she said, "but I don't think it would be advisable for you to come in right now. There are two of Richard's associates with him, and the conversation just turned to Dr. Morthley and U.N.C.L.E. They seem quite bitter."

"Speak of the devil," Napoleon said. "You mean it's not just your husband who has suddenly decided that U.N.C.L.E. is basically evil?"

"Oh, no. Sometimes I think it's the whole town. Yesterday I even heard Richard talking to the boy who delivers our groceries. Maybe the boy was just being polite, but it didn't sound that way."

"Do you have any idea what happened to change them?" Napoleon asked. "Your husband worked for us several times before."

"I know," she said. "When we got the first letter about a month ago, I assumed he would work for you this time. Now that I think back, he'd been acting strangely for a short time previously, but I hadn't paid any attention. This time he just ignored the letter, but the next one seemed to annoy him. Finally, when Willard phoned last week, he seemed to go off the deep end. Since then he's been ranting about U.N.C.L.E. to everyone he meets."

"But do you know what changed him?" Napoleon persisted. "You obviously don't feel this way yourself."

"No, I can't imagine what could have changed him. Of course, I was sick for some time; I wasn't noticing much. I'm over it now, except for a strict diet and avoiding exercise. The doctor said I'm as good as new. But apparently the change came while I was still in bed."

"He's never mentioned anything specific to you?" Napoleon asked.

"Nothing. I'm not even sure what he dislikes about U.N.C.L.E. He never says anything specific."

"Could we see him?" Illya asked, moving toward the door. "Perhaps he'd tell us what's troubling him."

Mrs. Armden shook her head. "I'm afraid you'd just make him worse."

"We'll have to see him some time, Mrs. Armden," Napoleon said politely. "We've driven almost a thousand miles. Mr. Waverly and Dr. Morthley are very concerned about him."

She silently debated with herself before answering. "Very well, I suppose you must. But try not to . . ." Her voice trailed off for a moment before she continued. "I hope you can help."

"We'll do our best," Napoleon assured her.

Mrs. Armden gave the impression of squaring her shoulders as she turned to open the door and lead the two agents into the house. They stopped in an archway leading to a comfortable-looking living room. A small, wiry man with a bristling gray crewcut rose from an armchair to greet them. Two other men, both younger, remained seated on a couch.

"Richard," Mrs. Armden said to the older man, "these are friends of Willard. They've come all the way from New York to . . ."

"From U.N.C.L.E., you mean?" Armden said shortly. "Some people just won't take no for an answer."

"We do work for U.N.C.L.E.," Napoleon admitted, "but we are here because we're friends of Dr. Morthley."

"Who also works for U.N.C.L.E.," Armden said, unimpressed. "I used to be a friend of his, until he was subverted by his other alleged friends." He laughed shortly. "I always thought he would have better sense than to be taken in by your kind."

"But you also used to work for us," Napoleon pointed out. "You seem to be the one who has changed, not Dr. Morthley."

Armden's face froze for a second, then, as if something had clicked in his mind, he began speaking rapidly. "That was before I knew the truth about you. Now that I know, I'm through. You'll never get me back into that den of murderers!"

"Interesting," Napoleon commented, watching Armden. "How did you find out the truth?"

"I'm sure you'd like to know," Armden said. "Then you could stop other people from learning about you. But you're too late; it's becoming common knowledge. Now then, I have better things to do with my time than waste it on you. If you will leave, I can get back to my real friends."

Armden turned his back on them and sat down with finality. The other two men smiled approvingly at him. "Don't waste our time," one of them said. "Run back to Mr. Waverly and tell him that U.N.C.L.E. doesn't fool us out here."

The two agents glanced at one another. Mrs. Armden stood behind them, looking nervous.

"That would seem to be that," Illya remarked.

Napoleon nodded agreement and turned to go. Mrs. Armden scurried along the hallway and opened the door. Back on the porch, Napoleon asked, "How long has this been going on? You said something about his acting strangely before he received our letters."

"I can't say when it began; I was sick and he was worried, and neither of us was behaving normally. I noticed some—oddities—in his actions. Whatever it was, I just assumed that he had a problem at work. There wasn't anything really definite until the letters arrived. Since then, it seems to have been getting steadily worse."

"And he's never been any more specific than he was tonight?"

"Never." She laughed nervously.

Napoleon looked thoughtful. "If we're going to find out anything useful, it's going to take more than this evening. Can you recommend a good hotel, Mrs. Armden?"

"There's only one hotel in town. It's just north of the square." She pointed vaguely northeast.

"Thank you," Napoleon said. "We'll be in touch with you again before the weekend is over."

She didn't seem overjoyed at the prospect, but she managed a weak smile as they walked to the car. Napoleon motioned Illya into the driver's seat and pulled out his communicator as he slid into the passenger's side.

"Yes, Mr. Solo?" Waverly's voice came to them as the car pulled away from the curb. "I've been waiting to hear from you. Have you communicated with Dr. Armden?"

"I don't think that's quite the right term. We talked with him briefly, but I don't think we communicated with him."

"That's hardly unusual in the world today, Mr. Solo. I sometimes think that's one of our biggest problems; great amounts of talk but no communication. But that's neither here nor there, is it? What seems to be the matter with Dr. Armden?"

"It's hard to say," Napoleon began. "It was a little like talking to a politician who has a set of platitudes but no real knowledge. We couldn't get him to give a direct answer." He recounted their meeting with Armden and his friends.

"So the unfriendliness isn't restricted to Dr. Armden," Waverly mused. "I was afraid of that. Do you know if these other people have influenced him, or have they, too, been acted on by some mysterious force?"

23

"Mrs. Armden gave the impression that no one individual was responsible for influencing her husband. We plan to stay here overnight and investigate further. Tomorrow will be Saturday, and we can reach most of the people we want to see. Perhaps we'll have more definite information for you then."

"Very well, Mr. Solo. There is one other person you might particularly want to speak to. Dr. Arnold Bennett is also employed by Falco, and he also once did some work for us." Waverly paused for a second before continuing. "Approach Dr. Bennett with caution, and keep me informed of the results. This begins to look a trifle sinister."

"Thrush, sir?" Napoleon speculated.

"Perhaps. It wouldn't do any harm to find if Dr. Armden's dislike for U.N.C.L.E. is accompanied by a corresponding fondness for Thrush. However, I don't want my agents to work on the assumption that Thrush is at the root of every problem. There are other inimical forces in the world. Remember to keep an open mind, Mr. Solo."

"Are there any local U.N.C.L.E. agents we could contact for information?" Napoleon asked.

Waverly thought for a moment. "The nearest major office would be Chicago, I believe. We have an office in Fort Wayne, but it's quite small; only one full-time agent. I seem to recall one or two part-time agents near Midford; we have several scattered throughout northern Indiana. Their duty is primarily information-gathering, but they might be able to render you some assistance, particularly since information is precisely what we are after here. I'll have a check made, and give you a list of names and addresses the next time you check in."

"Right, sir," Napoleon said. "I'll report in as soon as we've talked with Dr. Bennett. Solo out."

Napoleon replaced the communicator in his pocket

and settled back in the seat. *Another typical U.N.C.L.E. vacation,* he thought. *Relax and enjoy yourself, and keep your eyes open for any Thrushes who happen to be vacationing in your vicinity.*

Chapter 2

"The Hardest Part Is Finding A Rose With Hips"

DR. BENNETT LIVED ON a street bordering the Midford University campus. Illya insisted that they walk and enjoy the Hoosier autumn. They spotted Bennett's house from a block away, Bennett out on the lawn.

The man looked up from a lawn mower as they approached. "You still around?" he asked sharply. "What are you after now?"

"You're Dr. Arnold Bennett?" Napoleon asked.

"Yes, if it's any of your business."

"We understand you've done work for U.N.C.L.E. in the past, Dr. Bennett. We wondered why your attitude is so different now."

"I've come to my senses, is all," Bennett said impatiently.

"What's your opinion of Thrush?" Illya put in quickly.

"Thrush?" Bennett looked at them uncomprehendingly. "I'm a chemist, not a birdwatcher. Good day!" He gave the mower a vicious shove that almost ran it over Illya's foot, then turned and moved away across the lawn.

"I'm glad he doesn't have a power mower," Illya remarked as he watched Bennett disappear around the house into the back yard.

Napoleon was looking across the street at the campus. "Remember what Mrs. Armden said last night, about sometimes thinking the whole town had changed? Let's check someone from out of town."

"And let's hope Armden and friends haven't been broadcasting our description," Illya said as they started across the street.

In the middle of a small area of trees and carefully mowed grass stood a middle aged, portly gentleman, peering about with a distracted air. He looked up as the two agents approached.

"Have either of you gentlemen chanced to see a stray wombat this morning?" he asked, smiling uncertainly.

Napoleon looked startled. "I don't think so; what does a wombat look like?"

"Like a groundhog with delusions of grandeur," Illya explained and turned to their new acquaintance. "No, we haven't seen one. Is one missing?" Napoleon remained silent and made believe he knew what a groundhog looked like.

"Yes, Eyre seems to have vanished again," the portly man replied. "We named him Eyre because he's a long distance traveler; he's gotten loose before. He always comes back, of course, but he can cause rather expensive damage if we don't find him in time."

"Damage?" Napoleon asked.

"Wombats dig," Illya informed him.

Their portly acquaintance chuckled. "That's rather like saying that Hitler was a troublemaker, you know," he said. "A bit of an understatement, that is. Yes, they dig. They tend to undermine things." He glanced at the building near them. "Does the science building look a trifle tilted to you? No, that's ridiculous. But he must be around here somewhere."

"I'm afraid we wouldn't be of much help in a wombat hunt," Napoleon explained.

"Oh, yes, of course. You didn't come over here to help me hunt Eyre, so you must have come for some other reason. Deductive reasoning, you know. Now then, my name is Epaminondas T. Dodd; I'm head of the biology department here at Midford. Can I help you in any way?"

"Why, yes," Napoleon replied glibly, "I'm looking for a good, solid university for my nephew."

"Oh, I'm sure that Midford can fulfill any expectations," Dodd said. "You really should see President McLaughlin, but he's gone today. I suppose I could show you the science building."

"That seems fair enough," Napoleon said. "I'm merely making a preliminary report."

"Very well; come along. Since Eyre isn't about the grounds, we'll have to notify the Midford police department to be on the lookout for him. Sometimes I wonder if the prestige of being one of the few American universities to own a live wombat is really worth the trouble he causes."

They walked toward the building. "University life these days is so disruptive," said Napoleon. "Respect for authority is becoming a thing of the past. I hope that here at least it might be different. My brother is quite insistent on a good conservative college for his son."

"Oh, I'm sure Midford is conservative enough for you," Dodd assured him. "Just a few of the students tend to get out of hand now and then. Argue for student-privileges, write letters to the newspapers, read Henry Miller—that sort of thing. But the majority of our students are solid, hardworking types."

"I've heard, though," said Illya, "that a member of your faculty has given his services on occasion to some liberal international outfit in New York—U.N.C.L.E., I think it's called."

Dodd nodded. "I suppose that would be Professor Curtis. He's in the psychology department, and you know they're inclined to be a bit more liberal than we in the sciences. But I really doubt that he will be working with them again."

"Oh?" Napoleon looked interested. "Why?"

"Well, I couldn't say about that," Dodd replied. "We don't move in the same circles, you know. But last week there was a memorandum sent around by President McLaughlin, saying that members of the faculty were forbidden to accept outside employment with any organizations whose policies were inconsistent with the goals of the University. There was a list of forbidden organizations, and I'm sure U.N.C.L.E. was one of them." Dodd looked a little puzzled. "Personally I never heard of U.N.C.L.E.—or most of the others on the list. But conservatively speaking, I'm sure you can see that your nephew will be in good hands here."

Napoleon smiled ingratiatingly. "I'm sure he would, but would it be possible to speak to Professor Curtis?"

Dodd consulted his watch. "I think so. He's usually in his office on Saturday mornings. I can introduce you, if you can wait a few minutes until I phone about Eyre."

"No need to trouble yourself," said Napoleon.

"He doesn't seem familiar with Thrush," Illya remarked as they started across the campus, following his directions. "Either they aren't involved, or they're keeping well under cover."

When they found Professor Curtis he was grading tests while a girl across the desk from him was making a tabulation of some kind from another stack of papers. Napoleon introduced himself and Illya, then repeated his story about a fictitious nephew. Then he mentioned the memorandum that Dodd had told them about.

Curtis nodded pleasantly. "I don't understand what Gaspar thinks he's up to. I'm the only faculty member who has ever worked for U.N.C.L.E. or any of the other organizations on his fool list, and he knows that I'm not going to pay any attention to it. I suppose it's all part of a deal to get another donation from someone."

"You mean if U.N.C.L.E. asked you to help them out, you'd do it, in spite of the memorandum?" Napoleon looked mildly disapproving.

"Of course I would. In the first place, U.N.C.L.E. pays its research consultants very well."

Napoleon and Illya exchanged startled glances.

"In the second place," Curtis continued, oblivious of his visitors' amazement, "what I do with my spare time is my own business." Curtis reached into a desk drawer, pulled out a bottle containing a pale liquid, and took a drink.

"Rutabaga juice," he explained. "I'd offer you some, but it tastes terrible. Very nourishing, however; I always have some in the middle of the morning. Much healthier than those abominations you get from the soft drink machines on campus."

"I take it you're an advocate of health foods," Napoleon said. "Yoghurt, wheat germ, that sort of thing?"

Curtis threw back his head and laughed, a full throated sound that didn't seem to go with his small, wiry frame. "You forgot to mention blackstrap molasses. I've often wondered why the general public picked those particular items as representative of health foods, when there are so many others with less repellent names and superior nutritive value. Some of them even taste good. Take rose hip extract, for example. I'll be making some next week; they hit their peak vitamin content in October, you know."

Napoleon nodded sagely. "I suppose the hardest part is finding a rose with hips."

Curtis chuckled politely. "Rose hips are simply the seed pods of the rose. Properly prepared, rose hip extract provides as much vitamin C per glass as you can get from one hundred glasses of orange juice."

"Fascinating," Illya said, "but ..."

"Of course," Curtis continued, "while I prefer my own preparations, I haven't the time or the raw materials, so to speak, to prepare all my own food. I buy most of it. If you're interested, I have some literature. This rutabaga juice," he eyed the bottle critically, "comes from Irwin Vita-Glo, and seems decidedly inferior."

"This is all very interesting," Napoleon said desperately, "but it's not really why we came." He noted that the girl was fighting a losing battle to keep from laughing.

Curtis noticed her expression, and ceased his dissertation on health foods. "One giggle out of you," he warned the girl, "and I'll drop your grades ten points. I'm sorry gentlemen; I tend to become overenthusiastic about health foods. Rita, here, tends to restrain me. Just what was it you wanted to see me about?"

Napoleon hesitated, then took the plunge. He held out his identification card for Curtis' inspection. Rita moved closer in order to see the card herself.

Curtis read the card and sat back. "So your dear nephew was a figment of your imagination, and you're an U.N.C.L.E. agent, not an uncle. All right, what are you after?"

Napoleon explained their mission, and the anti-U.N.-C.L.E. feeling they had encountered. Curtis looked puzzled.

"That seems odd," he said. "I wouldn't attach much significance to old Gaspar's memo; he's always doing something like that, usually to impress a prospective donor. I wouldn't be surprised to find that he picked the organization names at random out of a current newspaper. But Armden and Bennett are different. The last time I spoke to Armden we were comparing notes on the work we had done for U.N.C.L.E. He seemed quite friendly then, though a bit concerned about breaking security."

"When was this?" Illya wanted to know.

Curtis pondered a moment. "Sometime during the summer term, I'm sure. Falco was thinking of instituting some kind of psychological testing in the personnel department and I was asked for some advice. I poked around the plant, looked profound, and asked questions. I remember that I was surprised to find someone else here who had worked with U.N.C.L.E."

"Can you think of any reason for them to change so suddenly?" Napoleon inquired. "Any anti-U.N.C.L.E. publicity in town recently?"

Curtis shook his head. "I don't think so. I haven't been keeping up with the local events. I've been busy with a survey of the behavior patterns of the university students, trying to find some correlation between their academic accomplishments and other behavioral characteristics." He grinned suddenly. "I haven't found anything, but I need to have something published professionally in the near future, so you can bet I'll find a correlation somewhere. I just haven't uncovered the right statistics yet."

Rita had been looking pensive. "This may not have anything to do with what you're after," she said, "but ever since I returned to school this fall—I had a summer job in New York—I've had an odd feeling about a lot of people. Not the students so much as the local people, and some of the faculty. There's a certain aloofness I never noticed before."

"Anything specific?" Napoleon asked quickly.

"Not really," she said, frowning. "I've been working with some of the local charities. I've noticed that donations have been falling off this fall. Fund drives don't raise as much, and people who sign up for payroll deductions, withdraw almost immediately. One recent drive only made 50% of its quota."

"That doesn't sound like Thrush," said Illya. "They'd set up a phony charity if they thought it would benefit them, but I can't see any profit for them in this."

Curtis had been listening intently to Rita's disclosure, his eyes gradually lighting up. "I hadn't realized it was such a widespread phenomenon," he said happily. "Do you really suppose there's any connection between anti-U.N.C.L.E. feeling and decreasing charitable donations? Maybe I won't need this statistical correlation after all. This could be a rare opportunity. There are, of course, many instances of an individual's going through a profound psychological change, but I don't recall any record of an entire town doing it."

Curtis broke off to hum a few bars of something that vaguely resembled "Hot Time In The Old Town Tonight," then rubbed his hands together gleefully. He seemed to have forgotten Illya and Napoleon completely.

"Let's see. I don't believe a printed questionnaire would achieve the best results in this case. Perhaps I could make it a project for my classes. Hmmmm. . . Each student would have to cover—oh, half a dozen families, if we restricted the study to Midford itself. It shouldn't take more than a week or so." Curtis was pacing furiously now. "Yes, that should be the best approach. We can work out a list of questions and get it mimeographed—"

Curtis halted suddenly. "I'm sorry, gentlemen," he apologized, "but this is an unusual opportunity. Just think of it: an entire town!"

"I quite understand," Napoleon assured him. "In fact, we would be very much interested in the outcome. And, if you don't mind the suggestion of an outsider, could you possibly include a question about Thrush in your survey? It could be a great help."

"Ah, yes, a bird in the hand, so to speak. Certainly, certainly. After all, it was you who brought the matter to my attention. Perhaps you would like to look over the survey questions before we run them off? Why don't you stop by tomorrow afternoon if you're still in town? I should have the questions worked out."

Illya started to say something, but Curtis rushed on. "The first thing, of course, is to win their confidence, so we'll need a couple of innocuous, ego-building questions first. And then . . ."

Napoleon and Illya exchanged glances, shrugged and departed. Rita gave them a solemn wink as she busily noted down Curtis' flood of ideas.

Chapter 3

"What's Your Excuse For Starting This Riot?"

THE REST OF THE DAY was uneventful. They spent most of the time wandering about the miniscule business district of Midford, listening carefully, occasionally striking up casual conversations on the subject of charity and internationalist organizations. The majority of the populace was positively indifferent to international organizations; the major topic in the marketplace was the new high school basketball coach. By evening, Illya and Napoleon had found only a dozen people who were openly hostile to U.N.C.L.E. However, no one was openly favorable; the general attitude seemed to be one of mild dislike.

Shortly after sunset, they drove to within a block of Armden's house, parked, and walked. The Sprite with the racing stripe was gone. This time Armden himself answered the door.

"Ah, the two intrepid agents again," he said, not offering to let them enter. "What are you after now? I thought I made myself clear yesterday."

"You did, on the subject of U.N.C.L.E." Napoleon asnwered. "We've been wondering just how you feel about Thrush?"

Armden laughed. "Arnold said you'd been around asking stupid questions this morning. I thought you'd get around to me, but I don't know any more about Thrush —I assume it's an organization?—than he does."

"All right," Napoleon acceded. "We would really like to know what happened to change your attitude toward U.N.C.L.E. We talked to Professor Curtis this morning, and he said you didn't feel this way this way a few months ago. And as we said to your wife last night, Dr. Morthley is quite concerned about you. You must have some kind of message for him, at least."

A flash of concern crossed Armden's face. "Poor Willard," he sighed. "He never was very sophisticated. It's easy to see how he could be taken in by an outfit like yours. Next thing he'll be donating valuable time to charity."

"You don't approve of charities?" Napoleon asked.

"The little ones are door-to-door beggars, and the big ones are swindlers." Armden snarled. "The entire idea is wrong, anyway. I made my own way without anybody's help, and other people can do the same. But the whole country is going downhill—look at us playing Santa Claus to a bunch of ignorant, ungrateful freeloaders without the guts to help themselves. Someone is going to have to take hold and bring this country to its senses." Armden paused, breathing heavily.

"But how does U.N.C.L.E. fit into this?" Illya asked.

"You're the worst of the lot! You put up this pose of international goodwill and friendship for everyone, and behind it—" he snorted.

"Yes," Napoleon prompted. "Behind it, what?"

"You don't know, of course!" Armden laughed derisively. "The innocent pose—you'd never admit anything!"

"But what should we admit to?" Napoleon persisted. "How did you find out?"

There was the same pause, as if a gearshift had fallen into place, that Napoleon had noticed the night before.

"Oh, I know you have a hand in the newspapers, the same way the government does. You never let any of your dirty laundry loose in public. Your killings are kept under wraps."

"You still haven't told us any specific thing that U.N.C.L.E. is supposed to have done." Napoleon argued.

Armden stood, unmoving, for several moments. Despite the coolness of the evening, Napoleon was sure he saw a bead of sweat form on the man's forehead. Suddenly he burst out. "You have no right to badger me this way! Get out of here and let me alone!" He spun on his heel and disappeared inside the house.

Napoleon and Illya walked quietly back to their car.

"I'm not sure I'd call it progress," Napoleon said. "But we seem to be hitting a nerve of some kind."

"At least he talked to us," Illya added. "He seemed more sympathetic toward Morthley. Perhaps we can try that approach again tomorrow."

"The more I see of this, the more it seems that Thrush must be involved. But how, and why?"

"You're just getting hypersensitive."

"Perhaps you're right, but I sense a plan in all this."

"What does it all mean?" Illya murmured as they drove back to the hotel.

Sunday afternoon Illya and Napoleon paid Dr. Armden another visit. Napoleon had barely touched the doorbell when the door popped open and Armden confronted them.

"Still here, I see." His voice was noticeably higher than it had been the night before, and there were shadows under his eyes.

"We'll probably be leaving tomorrow," Napoleon reassured him. "We just came by to make a final appeal.

We spoke to Dr. Morthley last night, and he is very concerned about you."

"Yes, I know. Willard called again this morning. He . . ." Armden broke off in midsentence and wiped his brow, then stood fidgeting for several seconds. The two agents waited patiently. Finally Armden continued, speaking rapidly. "Very well, gentlemen, I will call your bluff. I will go back to New York with you. But mind you, I'm doing this for Willard; I feel sure that once I see him in person, I can make him see the truth."

Illya and Napoleon exchanged glances. Their suggestion to Waverly the night before had evidently borne fruit. Now they would have to get Armden on his way before he changed his mind again, or any of his friends showed up to dissuade him.

"I'm glad to hear it, sir," Napoleon said. "If you haven't packed anything yet, just throw a few things together while we arrange for transportation. I'm sure we can make a flight from Fort Wayne."

Illya gestured toward the car after Armden had gone inside to pack. "That is not my idea of a three-passenger vehicle, unless we empty out the parachute compartment and stow someone in there."

"Armden is small," Napoleon replied. "Besides, would you rather give him the chance to talk to Bennett before leaving?" He contacted Waverly and was just completing the arrangements when Armden came out of the house carrying a small overnight case.

"I called the plant manager to let him know I won't be in for a couple of days," he informed them.

Napoleon winced slightly. "He didn't try to talk you out of it?"

"Of course not; why should he?"

"Just a thought," Napoleon said. "We've arranged for you to catch a six o'clock flight out of Fort Wayne." They headed for the car.

It took considerable maneuvering, but somehow both agents and Armden managed to fit into the car. Napoleon and Illya decided that the results would be endurable for a fifty-mile drive, and Armden seemed oblivious to the discomforts.

The drive was silent and uneventful. Armden seemed disinclined to talk, and both Napoleon and Illya felt the situation was too precarious to endanger it with idle conversation, since they didn't know what might serve to stir Armden up again. It was after five o'clock when they pulled into the airport parking lot, and Napoleon congratulated himself on having arrived in plenty of time. He was locking the car when someone tapped him on the shoulder. He deliberately finished turning the key in the lock before looking up. Instinctively he checked the location of Illya and Armden; they were standing on the other side of the car. A pudgy face confronted him from a distance of a few inches.

"You're with that U.N.C.L.E. outfit, ain't you?" the face demanded loudly. When Napoleon nodded, it continued.

"I thought I reckonized the car; they was an article about it in RODDING AND RAMMING." The face turned, and an arm motioned to someone in the background. "I told you it was them killers!"

Looking around, Napoleon saw half a dozen people converging on them. He motioned to Illya to get Armden away, but it was too late. The pudgy man who belonged with the face stuck out a beefy hand and grabbed Napoleon's shirt front, and at the same time the others moved toward Illya and Armden.

"It's U.N.C.L.E.!" a voice from somewhere shouted. "Let's show 'em what we do with their kind in a respectable town."

"Yeh!" the man grasping Napoleon said, snarling directly into his face. "We got a nice, clean city here, and we don't want you Commie killers even passing through. Just get back in your little wagon and move on." To emphasize the point, he gave Napoleon a vicious shove back against the car.

Out of the corner of his eye, Napoleon spotted something flying through the air. He ducked as whatever it was clattered noisily on the concrete of the parking lot. More people were gathering, now. Some were merely interested spectators, but many were starting to shout abuse. Napoleon knew enough about mob psychology to know that even the interested spectators would probably join in once the excitement built up.

He ducked again. This time it looked like an empty beer can. Looking up, he noticed that Illya and Armden were effectively blocked from returning to the car. Illya was trying to force a way through to the terminal building, but was encountering stiff resistance. Armden seemed to be in the passive state which had dominated him ever since entering the car, but he was following Illya.

If this crowd was feeling anything like Armden had felt Friday evening, there was no point in trying to argue with it. At the same time, he had a nasty vision of what U.N.C.L.E.'s midwestern image would be if he used the tear gas "pen" in his pocket on a crowd of innocent citizens. The tear gas had better be strictly a last resort. He began working his way toward Illya and Armden.

The pudgy man grabbed at him but missed. Another man, smaller, suddenly lurched forward into his path, as if he had been shoved. Napoleon avoided him just in time to duck another missile. He had almost reached Illya when someone lunged against him from behind. He sprawled against the side of a car, banging his shoulder painfully on the rear view mirror. All the time the voices were growing louder and more numerous.

By now, judging from the sound, the largest part of the crowd didn't know what it was yelling about, but was simply letting off steam. A group of teen-age boys had started pushing one another.

He struggled to his feet, leaning against the car. The teen-agers were abruptly leaving. Looking in the direction opposite to their flight, Napoleon saw a policeman coming from the airport terminal. Nearby, Illya was regaining his feet.

The crowd was beginning to break up. The pudgy man was nowhere to be seen. In fact, Napoleon suddenly noticed, none of the group which had formed the nucleus of the mob was anywhere around. The people now making way for the officer were the interested bystanders who had joined the mob at its height. Looking around, he noticed something else.

"Illya!" he called. "Where's Armden?"

Illya looked around hastily. "I don't know," he called back. "He was right behind me when we started for the terminal; I thought he was still with me."

Napoleon vaulted onto the hood of the car nearest him, stepped to the roof, and looked around for Armden. The bristly gray crewcut was nowhere in sight. Illya by now was on another car roof, also searching.

"Okay, get down from there!" The policeman was standing belligerently beside the car Napoleon was on. The remnants of the crowd were disappearing.

Napoleon took a last look around and clambered down.

"You, too!" the officer bellowed at Illya, who leaped nimbly to the ground. "All right now, let's see some identification!"

"I'm certainly glad to see you," Napoleon said, reaching for his wallet. "There was another man with us, who—"

"Never mind the chatter, let's see some identification!"

Napoleon sighed, and proffered his wallet. Illya

walked over and extended his U.N.C.L.E. card. The officer scowled.

"U.N.C.L.E., eh? All right, what's your excuse for starting this riot?"

"We didn't start it," Napoleon explained. "We were very nearly its victims."

"Uh-huh. I've heard that one before. If you weren't agitating, what were you doing on top of cars? Get a move on."

"But, officer," Napoleon protested. "There was a third man with us who disappeared during the confusion. We were merely looking for him."

"Third man, huh? I don't see any third man around." By now the crowd had entirely vanished. "What were you doing here?"

"We were bringing this other man to the airport. There's a reservation on the next flight for him."

"Okay, where's your car?"

With a sinking feeling, Napoleon pointed to the U.N.-C.L.E. car. The officer stared at it for several seconds before turning back to him.

"Oh, there was a third man with you, was there? And you came in that car. All right, now; do you two get out of here, or do I run you in for disturbing the peace? If I didn't hate making reports, I'd have you booked by now."

Napoleon glanced at Illya, who shrugged. Under the watchful eye of the policeman, they got into the car and headed for the exit. Once outside the parking lot, Illya pulled the car off the road and stopped.

"I wish the C.I.A. hadn't made people so suspicious of security organizations," he commented.

Napoleon got out. "Stay with the car," he advised. "One man will be less conspicuous and I'd sooner have one of us mobile in case of more trouble." Keeping a sharp eye out for pudgy citizens and policemen, he walked back to the terminal building.

Armden was nowhere in sight. After a brief search, Napoleon approached the ticket counter. The girl was very polite, but not too helpful. Yes, a reservation had been made for a Dr. Armden, but it had not been claimed, and the flight was boarding now. No, she had not seen a middle-aged man with a gray crewcut. Napoleon thanked her, rejoined Illya in the car, and contacted Waverly. The latter was doubly upset over the loss of Dr. Armden and the worsening U.N.C.L.E. image in the midwest.

"I suppose you'll simply have to look for him," Waverly concluded. "From your description of his state of mind, he may be anywhere."

"I hope so," Napoleon said. "Although that mob formed and broke up just a bit too quickly for my peace of mind. I keep having the nasty suspicion that it broke up because it had done its job."

"Could you check and see if Dr. Armden had any friends in Fort Wayne?" Illya inquired. "He could have decided that he wanted to convert them, as he planned to convert Dr. Morthley when he got to New York. He didn't appear to be too rational."

Waverly considered the idea. "Perhaps you're right, Mr. Kuryakin. At least, it will give you a place to start looking. Stand by."

It turned out that Dr. Armden had a good dozen friends or colleagues in the Fort Wayne area, and it was late by the time the agents had contacted them all and explained the situation. Nothing was learned; Armden hadn't seen any of them for several months. They checked in again with Waverly, who could only sound regretful and urge them to get a good night's sleep before renewing the search Monday morning.

But the renewed search was not necessary. Napoleon was roused from a sound sleep Monday morning by the warbling of his communicator. Waverly informed him that Mrs. Armden had just called to say that her husband had returned the night before, acting rather strangely, and that he had just gone back to work as if nothing had happened.

Chapter 4

"Habit, Nothing But Habit"

JUST AFTER 9:30, Napoleon and Illya pulled into the visitor's parking lot at Falco Industries. A uniformed guard greeted them politely at the plant entrance and let them in as far as a little railed waiting area next to his desk. Their hesitant admission that they were U.N.C.L.E. agents brought no change in the guard's attitude, and he promised to try and have Dr. Armden located for them.

This was apparently the entrance to a manufacturing area; through a pair of wide swinging doors they could hear the rumble of machinery. As the two agents waited, four men in jeans and faded chambray shirts pushed through the doors and clustered in front of a group of vending machines directly across from the waiting area. After a minute spent in flipping coins, the loser began depositing dimes in the coffee machine. The first man to pull a cup from behind the little window put it to his lips and sipped cautiously. After a second, he made a face that lay somewhere between everyday disapproval and mild nausea.

"Better than usual," he said.

"It's Monday morning," one of the others said as he reached for the second cup. "It hasn't had time to ferment yet." He took a small swallow and grimaced slightly. "You're right; it isn't half bad today."

The third man made a similar face when he got a cup from the soft drink machine next to the coffee.

"Habit, nothing but habit," he grumbled. "They could put lighter fluid in here and we'd drink it."

The last man was pondering his choice when the guard hung up the phone and turned to the two agents. "They can't seem to locate Dr. Armden. He isn't in his office."

"He is in the plant, however?" Napoleon asked.

"Sure, he's here somewhere. Saw him come in myself, earlier than usual. Working on some hot project, I guess. He's probably out checking on something."

"Could we speak with his boss?" Napoleon wanted to know.

"I dunno; I'll see." The guard returned to the phone. "Put me through to John Kilian, will you, Hazel?" He waited briefly, then resumed talking. "Mr. Kilian? I've got two men out here. They wanted to talk to Armden, but we couldn't locate him. They asked to talk to you." There was another pause. "All right." He turned to Napoleon and Illya, extending the telephone. "He'll talk to you."

Napoleon took the receiver. "Mr. Kilian? My name is Napoleon Solo. I wounder if you could answer a few questions about Dr. Armden?"

There was a quiet chuckle from the other end of the line. "If you guarantee you aren't recruiting for another company. If you are, you'll have to contact our personnel department. We aren't allowed to give out information directly."

"In a manner of speaking, I suppose I am. I represent U.N.C.L.E. and we had hoped to get Dr. Armden's services as a consultant in a certain matter. He agreed to come to New York, but then left us at the Fort Wayne airport yesterday. We'd like to know why he changed his mind so suddenly."

"Oh, you're the ones. I couldn't tell you why he changed his mind; he called me yesterday afternoon and said he was going, and then this morning he showed up here, ready to go to work on his latest project. I will say, though," the voice took on a formal tone, "that I was quite surprised when he informed me that he was going with you. He has spoken of U.N.C.L.E. recently, and not at all favorably."

"Has Dr. Armden been acting normally today? His wife said he was acting rather strangely last night."

"You've spoken to Mrs. Armden, then?"

"Only indirectly, but—"

"I'm afraid that's all the information I can give you." Kilian's voice became even more formal. "When I see Richard, I'll tell him you were here. Now let me speak with the guard again."

Napoleon frowned slightly and obediently handed the phone to the guard, who listened silently for several seconds and hung up with a crisp "Yes, sir."

"I have the feeling we're about to be ordered out," Napoleon remarked to Illya as he watched the guard turn toward them.

"Ah, the two spies again! How nice to see you." Sascha Curtis bustled around his desk and held out his hand. "What can I do for you today?"

"We have a new problem for you," Napoleon informed him. "If you can spare the time from your survey."

"Certainly. I don't have another class for an hour. What sort of problem did you have in mind?"

"Dr. Armden," Napoleon informed him. "Yesterday he decided to visit Dr. Morthley in New York. We got him as far as the Fort Wayne airport, where he disappeared. Somehow, he got back here to Midford last night. His wife said he was acting strangely."

"Strangely? How?"

"He walked in the door last night and went to bed with hardly a word. Then this morning he was up earlier than usual and off to Falco almost an hour early. Apparently he simply ignored her questions."

Curtis looked thoughtful. "Very interesting. That, plus the apparent personality change, points to some type of schizophrenia."

"Would a split personality really explain all his actions?" Napoleon asked.

"It might. Secondary personalities are often not fully developed and seem very dull when compared with the primary personality. However, only the most spectacular schizophrenics develop true split personalities. Most simply have a fixed delusion on some subject."

"Such as thinking U.N.C.L.E. is an international Communist plot?" Illya inquired.

"That could well be one aspect," Curtis said. "There would almost certainly be others, though."

"He's decided that charities are either useless or criminal," Napoleon offered.

Curtis nodded. "Any radical change from his former personality could be a part of it. I don't know what his previous feelings were about charities, but judging from your description, his present feelings are a bit extreme."

Illya frowned. "But schizophrenia isn't contagious."

"I had always assumed it was not. But, then, until yesterday I always assumed that stories of entire towns suffering personality changes were nonsense. Now . . ." Curtis shrugged. "We'll see what the survey has to say about it. Incidentally, I've been talking to a few of the faculty since Saturday. It isn't Gaspar and his memo that are anti-U.N.C.L.E. Half a dozen of the instructors practically had apoplexy at the mention of U.N.C.L.E. I told them a year ago that swilling all that pop and coffee would rot their brains as well as their stomachs— that was when they put those infernal vending machines in the Student Union. But nobody listens to a psychologist. Anyway, there is also a small but vocal group of students who have been orating against U.N.C.L.E. and international plots in general. Oddly, these aren't the type of students who usually go in for this sort of thing. Not a intellectual—genuine or phony—in the lot. In fact, a good many of them were attending summer school this year to make up courses they flunked last spring."

"And the most outspoken U.N.C.L.E. critics off campus are two of the most capable and intelligent men in town: Armden and Bennett," Illya said.

"A very interesting problem," Curtis said happily. "I wonder if the source—if there is a source—is in the University or the town. Or is it common to both? A most stimulating problem."

Neither agent had the heart to mention their experiences in Fort Wayne. If Curtis had thought the problem was that widespread, he would go into such a transport of ecstasy that not even his rose hip extract could save him. Instead, they turned his attention back to Dr. Armden.

"I'd love to speak to him," said Curtis. "Do you think you could arrange it?"

"Nothing easier," Napoleon assured him. "Meet us at his house this evening. We'll check with his wife ahead of time, but I'm sure she'd like to have you see him. She seems quite concerned for his sanity."

"Fine, fine." Curtis rubbed his hands together briskly. He glanced at his wrist watch. "Now you'll have to excuse me; my first class should be back with the results of their first day's questioning any minute now." He bounced around his desk and drew a cylindrical container from one of the drawers. "Would you care for some Bulgarian yoghurt?" he asked as he removed the lid. "I believe it's chocolate-peach today." He sniffed the aroma from the open container. "Delicious!"

Both agents maintained expressions of cordiality until they closed Curtis's door behind them. They kept respectfully silent and tried to think kind thoughts as they walked toward their car. By use of stern self-control, Illya even managed to avoid being sick on the campus lawn.

The front door opened and Mrs. Armden appeared to greet them. They introduced Professor Curtis. Napoleon asked if Dr. Armden had improved any since morning.

Mrs. Armden looked a little grim. "He at least answers direct questions now. At the moment, he's just sitting there staring at the TV set. At a program he *never* watches."

The three men followed her to the living room. Armden sat on a couch, blankly watching the TV set. He didn't look up as they entered the room.

"Richard, we have visitors," Mrs. Armden said hesitantly.

Armden continued to stare at the TV screen for several seconds, then turned slowly to face them. Recognition was similarly delayed. "Mr. Solo and Mr. Kuryakin," he said, speaking slowly and distinctly. "I should apologize for yesterday; even an U.N.C.L.E. agent deserves common courtesy. I simply realized I was wasting my time and decided to return."

"This is Professor Curtis, from the university," Mrs. Armden said.

Armden rose and extended his hand deliberately to Curtis. "I remember you. You were at the plant last summer for a day or two."

"I remember you quite well, too, Dr. Armden. We compared notes on our work for U.N.C.L.E." Curtis was watching Armden intently.

Armden frowned. "I had forgotten that. I suppose you are working with these two men now?"

"Not really," Curtis answered. "I'm working on a survey for the university, and—"

Curtis broke off as Armden turned from him to face the TV set. Nobody had turned the volume down, and a particularly loud commercial had just come on. "Don't wait another minute!" an announcer's voice was exhorting. "Go down to the nearest Gackenheimer's store and take advantage of this incredible, once-in-a-lifetime offer! You can't afford not to take advantage of it. There are Gackenheimer's stores in Bippus, Midford, East Manchester, and Hunterton, and they're all open tonight until 9:00!"

Armden turned away from the set and started into the hallway. His wife held out a hand to him. "Where are you going?" she asked.

"To the store," he said without pausing.

"Gackenheimer's? But that's a feed and grain store! We never bought anything there in our lives!"

Armden approached the front door, still in his shirt sleeves, and reached for the knob. Illya had been watching him closely and now spoke sharply.

"Dr. Armden, come back here!"

Armden hesitated.

"Come back in here!" Illya repeated, more loudly.

This time Armden stopped, halfway through the door. Slowly he turned and came back toward the living room. Curtis darted over to the TV set and shut it off, then stood nodding his head slowly.

"Sit down on the couch!" Illya commanded.

Armden obeyed wordlessly.

Illya glanced at Napoleon. "Thrush, anyone?" he asked. "Or do you know of any normally abnormal mental condition that would account for Armden's reactions?"

Curtis shook his head. "Hypnosis, or drugs," he said. "Certainly not schizophrenia; obeying orders is not a schizophrenic's strong point."

"Mrs. Armden." Illya turned to the woman, who had been standing with a stunned look ever since Armden had come back into the room. "I have no idea how, but your husband must be involved with Thrush. They've done something to him—drugs, hypnosis, something; we can't tell until he's been examined by qualified physicians. The best thing we could do now would be to get him to U.N.C.L.E. headquarters in New York where he'll be safe and we can have our doctors give him a complete examination."

Mrs. Armden began to look overwhelmed. She turned to Curtis.

"That would probably be best," he said. "He could be examined here, of course, but U.N.C.L.E. maintains an excellent medical staff, and they are more accustomed to this sort of thing."

"Besides," Napoleon added, "the way things are shaping up in Midford, we can't be sure the doctors aren't controlled by Thrush in some way."

She nodded silently to the two agents.

"Shall we try another order?" Illya asked, and without waiting for a reply, he turned to face Armden.

"Come with us to U.N.C.L.E. headquarters," he said, slowly and distinctly.

Armden stood up. "Very well," he said, and stood still, apparently awaiting further instructions.

"Mrs. Armden had better come, too," Napoleon said. "Thrush isn't averse to kidnapping close relatives to exert pressure on anyone they're interested in. Professor Curtis, would you do us a favor?"

"Of course," Curtis agreed immediately.

"We'll have to take Armden in our car." Napoleon saw Illya shudder at the thought of a thousand miles of driving with three people in the U.N.C.L.E. car. He continued. "We'll have to be with him to protect him. There are too many people saying things that could be dangerous if taken literally, which is apparently how Dr. Armden is going to take them. So, could you drive Mrs. Armden to the Fort Wayne airport? We'll arrange for a seat on the next flight to New York and for some of our people to meet her there. All you have to do is make sure she gets on the plane."

"Certainly," Curtis said.

"The sooner we get going, the better," Illya said. "Mrs. Armden, would you pack something for your husband and yourself? We won't have room for anything in the car, so you'll have to take all the clothing with you."

She nodded and turned to go upstairs. Illya spoke to Armden again. "Just come with us, Dr. Armden. Everything will be—"

Armden, who had been standing silently since Illya had first ordered him to come with them, suddenly screamed and lunged forward, swinging his fists wildly. Illya ducked and grabbed one arm. Napoleon quickly grasped the other.

"Do you have anything to quiet him down?" Illya asked as Armden struggled violently in their grip.

"In the car. Professor, take an arm and hang on until I get back."

Curtis hesitantly reached for the arm Napoleon was gripping. Armden was still struggling violently, but apparently hadn't thought about kicking yet. As Curtis tried to take over for Napoleon, however, Armden suddenly gave a second scream and went limp. The two agents lowered him gently to the couch. Illya hurriedly checked his pulse while Napoleon tried to calm Mrs. Armden. Curtis stood by, fascinated.

After a minute, Illya satisfied himself that Armden was merely unconscious. He picked up the slight form and turned to Napoleon, who had finally persuaded Mrs. Armden that the best thing to do was to get packed and go into hysterics later.

"Get the doors open," Illya admonished. "We have some packing of our own to do." He nodded at Armden's limp form.

Section II : "Harrass The Foe From The Rear"

Chapter 5

"How Does One Lose A Helicopter?"

DAWN, TO SOMEONE WHO has been awake for twenty-four hours and driving in an incredibly cramped car for eight, can be extremely bleak. Somewhere near the eastern end of the Ohio turnpike, Napoleon pulled to the side of the road and stopped next to a sign that read "Emergency Stop Only." He pushed up the gull-wing door and swung his feet out from under the steering wheel. Automatically taking the keys from the ignition, he stood up, stretched, stamped his feet a few times, and shook his head.

"You'd better take over again," he said to Illya, after a minute of the brisk autumn air had done nothing whatever in the way of shaking off the feeling of lethargy.

Illya obediently struggled out of the passenger's side, then stood there, leaning over, one hand propping up Dr. Armden. "Get over here and hang on to him," he said, a touch of irritation showing. "If I let go, he'll shift one way or the other and we'll be another half hour getting ourselves stuffed back in."

Napoleon hurried around the car and held Armden in place while Illya inserted himself beneath and behind the steering wheel. Once settled, he held Armden while Napoleon got in.

Illya glanced at the clear morning sky as he reached up to pull down the door. "This car even attracts attention from helicopters," he observed.

"Probably belongs to the highway department, or the local police," Napoleon answered, stifling a yawn. "Some places use them to check traffic flow." He closed his eyes.

"I think we're being followed," Illya said. "Either this one or one just like it was hovering over us the last time we stopped."

Napoleon pushed open his door and looked up. After a second, he spotted a noisy speck well up in the sky. It appeared to be hovering.

"And you didn't tell me? What kind of a friend are you?"

"A considerate one. We've no assurance that it is following us, and even if it is, what do you propose to do about it?"

Napoleon shrugged. "Nothing, I suppose. As long as it stays that high." He closed the door and his eyes almost simultaneously.

Illya drove silently. At the next stop for gas, there was a helicopter hovering overhead. They discussed the possibilities, and decided to stay on the turnpike. The side roads wouldn't hide them from aerial observation, and Napoleon thought they might be able to outrun a conventional helicopter on a straightaway. Also, there were several tunnels ahead.

The traffic had picked up, so neither Napoleon nor Illya immediately noticed the two large sedans that merged smoothly into traffic in front of them. Napoleon, who was driving, was only mildly irritated when the sedans pulled even with one another and blocked both lanes while moving slightly slower than he wanted to travel. After a few minutes of this, both cars began to slow down, still carefully abreast. At the same time, two similar cars appeared in his rear-view mirror, blocking both lanes behind him.

"It would seem," Napoleon said, nodding toward the cars ahead, "that they've called in the ground forces."

Illya put his head out the window and peered up. "The air force is closing in, too."

"This would seem to settle any doubts about Thrush being involved. No one else I know can afford massed ranks of cars *and* a helicopter to run us down. I hate to say I told you so, but . . ."

"But you'll make an exception for a friend; I know." Illya interrupted him.

Napoleon was driving carefully, watching the four cars. They were still slowing, and the two in back were drawing closer. Then one of the cars in the rear began to draw ahead of the other. Napoleon promptly swung the U.N.C.L.E. car in front of it, and it dropped back and its companion pulled ahead. By now they could hear the roar of the approaching helicopter.

"We're thoroughly boxed in," Napoleon reported. "Looks like they may try to run us off the road."

Illya looked calmly at the sheer drop a few feet from the right lane of traffic. "If we're going to be run off the road, I'd suggest getting into the left lane. The median strip is steep, but it may not be a total disaster. I wonder if they've given up trying to get Armden back alive?"

Napoleon swung into the left lane, and the following cars reversed their positions. He eyed the dash panel speculatively. "There must be something to use in a situation like this."

"With a dozen ordinary motorists in the line of fire," Illya suggested, "our choices are limited. I can just see the U.N.C.L.E. image after we've wiped a flame-thrower across a car full of innocent bystanders."

"And the laser system has the same drawback," Napoleon muttered. "At least the flame-throwers are a relatively short-range weapon. Still, we'd better have something; they're closing in fast."

He studied the road and the surrounding cars, and suddenly brightened. "This won't lose the helicopter," he announced, "but it won't damage the innocent bystanders, either."

A hundred yards ahead, a police crossover was built across the median strip. As they approached it, Napoleon's hand hovered over a button on the dash. Suddenly he stabbed the button, accelerated until he was directly behind the cars ahead, and then hit the brakes and swerved into the crossover. The cars behind disappeared into a thick cloud of smoke ejected from the rear of the U.N.C.L.E. car. Napoleon cut off the smoke screen as they bounced across the median strip and turned into the opposite lanes of the dual highway as angry motorists tooted irritably at them. Behind them, a section of the east bound lanes was blanketed by a dense smoke screen which was already beginning to dissipate. The four Thrush cars were moving slowly eastward, looking for a place to cross the median, while the cars behind honked at them for blocking traffic.

Napoleon had accelerated after crossing the median, but after seeing the success of his maneuver he slowed to keep the U.N.C.L.E. car in the normal traffic flow. A short while later an exit appeared, and Napoleon swung off the turnpike.

There was no sign of the Thrush cars as they pulled up to the toll booth, but the helicopter was an ominous speck in the sky. Rather than try to explain why they were in a westbound lane with an eastbound ticket, Napoleon confessed to losing his ticket, and paid for the entire distance.

"I can see you trying to explain that on your expense account," Illya commented.

"My expense account? It was your neck, too!"

"But you were driving," Illya pointed out. He looked up. "They're still with us."

"The copter must have spotted us and radioed ahead to set up the ambush," Napoleon said. "They can do the same thing again, though we'll have more boltholes on this sort of a road." He paused thoughtfully. "How does one lose a helicopter?"

"With great difficulty, I suspect," Illya said. He struggled to get turned around in the crowded quarters. "Open the weapons compartment, will you? I want to see what we have."

Napoleon pressed another button on the dash and a panel slid up, revealing a compartment behind it. Illya reached back into it, fished around for awhile, and brought out something that looked like the results of a violent collision between a target revolver and a small air gun.

Napoleon gave it a sidelong glance. "You've been playing with the new ordnance again," he accused. "That's one I haven't even seen."

"You should spend more time in the labs. This is a Mercox dart projectile gun."

"Dart?" Napoleon exclaimed. "I read about that fellow in the Congo who shot down a helicopter with a bow and arrow, but I didn't realize he'd made such an impression on our technical staff."

"Patience, Napoleon," Illya soothed. "This uses the gas from a blank cartridge to fire various projectiles: tear gas, dye marker, hypodermic darts, shaped charges —just about anything you want. The original gun is extremely versatile, and this one has been worked over somewhat by our lab boys." He rummaged through the weapons compartment again and triumphantly held up a handful of cartridges that looked like small rockets.

"Our HE-37 explosive, in a shaped charge that projects almost the entire force forward. It can do almost as much damage as a light field piece, if the opposition comes within range."

"I knew there was a catch to it," Napoleon commented. "What's the effective range?"

"About eighty yards, which is a bit more than the original version would do."

"Oh, fine. Don't shoot until you see the whites of their eyes. What about the rockets in the car doors?"

Illya considered. "Since they're fixed to fire horizontally, I don't think I'd want to try them against a helicopter unless we stop and take the door off. I know they have a heat-seeking device, but I'm afraid if we launched one here, it would be more likely to destroy a herd of cows than the helicopter."

"All right, then; the problem is to lure the copter close enough for you to use your hybrid there." Napoleon began to watch the roadside for an opportunity. The helicopter had descended to perhaps five hundred feet, where it remained.

In the next half hour, no opportunity presented itself. Then, just as both agents were beginning to wonder when the next covey of Thrushes would appear, the helicopter suddenly abandoned its cautious stalking and began to descend.

"Here they come," Illya said. "And unless I'm mistaken, they mean business."

As if to confirm Illya's suspicions, there was a rattling sound and a line of tiny pits appeared in the highway ahead of them. Napoleon swerved into the other lane and floored the accelerator. The firing stopped as the car pulled away. The car had more acceleration than the helicopter and on a straight road it would have had more speed. But they weren't on a straight road; in a few minutes, the helicopter pulled even with them again.

"Hang on!" Napoleon said as he spotted a side road that looked as though it ran through some fairly thick trees. He applied the brakes vigorously and skidded into the road.

"We're in luck," he said, eyeing the trees that lined both sides of the road and met in a multi-colored arch over their heads. For at least a few hundred yards, they were invisible from the air. Napoleon pulled off to one side of the road and stopped directly under one of the larger trees. He shut off the motor and climbed out of the car.

"Let's go down a few trees and see what happens when they find out we're not coming out the other end of the woods," he said, pulling his U.N.C.L.E. Special from its shoulder holster.

Illya followed, carrying the Mercox in one hand and stuffing projectiles into a pocket with the other. Judging from the sound, the helicopter was hovering a few hundred yards further down the road.

"Wait a minute," Illya said. "I'll need some help with this; come back and give me a boost."

Napoleon halted and looked around. Illya was standing at the base of a large tree, looking up into the branches. Napoleon walked back to him.

"It must be the country air," he said as he approached. "When we were looking for Dr. Morthley in Wisconsin last summer, you were constantly climbing trees. I think your ancestry is showing." He bent over to allow Illya to climb on his shoulders.

"This time you can stay on the ground," Illya sssured him. "Just don't shoot at the helicopter through the branches of this particular tree."

"Don't worry; I seldom shoot at things I can't see."

"Precisely why I'm climbing up here," Illya said, as he disappeared into the higher branches.

A minute later, the sound of the helicopter grew louder as it flew directly overhead. It apparently went back to the highway, then started slowly back along the road. The copter was almost over Illya's tree when he heard the loud whiplash crack of the Mercox. There was no following explosion; apparently Illya had missed. There was an answering fire from the helicopter, however. Trying to judge its location from the sound of the motor, he loosed several rounds through the branches of a tree about 20 yards from the one Illya was ensconced in. He ducked behind the trunk of the tree as several bullets rattled through the branches.

Almost simultaneously, there was a loud explosion from a nearby field. Napoleon whirled to stare, then relaxed as he realized that it was merely Illya's first round coming back down. He hoped there were no cows or farmers in the immediate vicinity.

The Mercox cracked a second time, and the sound of the shot was almost drowned out by the following explosion. The sound of the helicopter's engine changed immediately, shifting into a higher pitch as the gunner stopped firing. Then there was the sound of something crashing through the branches of the trees. A moment later, a large tubular piece of metal with a small rotor attached dropped with a clatter to the road. Illya came scrambling down from the tree.

"I shot the stabilizer off," he said, a mixture of smugness and surprise in his voice. "They may not crash right away, but they're going to be too dizzy to pay any attention to us."

Napoleon didn't reply. He hurried back to the car with Illya and looked admiringly at the Mercox as they repacked Armden.

Chapter 6

"What *Is* All This Stuff Under Here?"

WHAT SHOULD HAVE BEEN an easy six-hour trip on the turnpikes was on its way to becoming a twelve-hour endurance test on the regular and secondary highways of Pennsylvania. The fact that there were three of them stuffed into a car barely adequate for two made the situation that much worse. Until mid-afternoon, they had the advantage that Armden, jammed between the two agents, remained peacefully unconscious. Before they were through Pennsylvania, however, he woke up. His first words, after blinking and noting the crowded situation, were, predictably, "What happened? Where am I?"

Napoleon, who had been driving for the past fifty miles, slowed the car and prepared for whatever action Armden might be in the mood for. Illya reached in his pocket and closed his hand over the hypospray he had been keeping in readiness.

"You became ill when we were ready to leave for New York," Illya explained. "We decided to make the trip anyway, since it seemed you were in need of some specialized medical attention that we could provide." He watched Armden closely for any reaction.

"Ill?" Armden looked puzzled. "And we were about to leave for New York? But why . . ." His voice trailed off uncertainly and his brow wrinkled in frowning concentration. The two agents watched him carefully. After a minute his frown deepened. "I remember most of what happened," he said slowly, "but none of it makes any sense. I must have passed out."

"Yes, sir," Napoleon agreed. "What do you remember?"

"You two came last Friday, to find out why I had refused to . . ." Armden broke off incredulously. "But why should I have refused to help Willard Morthley? He's one of my oldest friends." He thought a moment, and went on. "When you came to the house, I was with Arnold Bennett, and—" He stopped, shaking his head. "Either I've just lost my mind, or I've been out of it for the past several weeks."

"I don't think so, sir," Illya assured him. "There have been other people acting the same way. Somehow, Thrush has been influencing you and a good portion of Midford. Professor Curtis suggested drugs or hypnosis, but that's only a guess. I can't imagine how a drug could have been administered to that many people, unless Thrush sprayed the entire town with a crop-duster. And hypnosis seems even more difficult."

"You might have something there," Napoleon broke in. "Thrush does have a fairly extensive air force."

"We hope you'll be able to help us find out how Thrush managed it," Illya continued. "You have no objections to a complete examination?"

Armden shook his head. "Of course not. Anything that would explain the past month is more than welcome."

The agents relaxed; Illya removed his hand from the pocket containing the hypospray.

"How are you feeling?" Napoleon inquired. "You've been out cold for almost a full day. Think some food would do you any good?"

Armden nodded. A few minutes later Napoleon pulled into a drive-in. He spotted a section with picnic style tables and nosed the car up next to one. The three men got out of the car, Armden staggering a bit at first. After stretching their muscles, they all walked up to the self-service window.

A few minutes later, they moved back to the table, having avoided answering most of the inevitable questions about the car that were invariably asked by the other customers. This sort of thing had happened at every stop, and the agents had by now developed a standard line of patter about cross country mileage tests and an experimental sports car. Illya usually pulled out a notebook and asked for the names of anyone who wanted to receive free literature about the car. This usually discouraged most curiosity seekers, who were hesitant about having their names added to still another mailing list, but occasionally he would have to take down some names and addresses.

This looked like one of the times the notebook would be required. There hadn't been many customers, and all but one had quietly gone back to their own cars when the list was brought up. That one, however, was on his way to becoming a problem. A polite description, Illya decided, would be "garrulous old coot."

"Mileage test?" he was saying skeptically as he sat down uninvited across the table from Illya. "Nobody that gives a damn about mileage is gonna buy one of these. Lemme see that notebook; I'll bet you didn't even write my name down." He reached across the table toward Illya, practically dragging his jacket sleeve in Illya's coffee.

Illya irritably flipped the notebook open to show the man his name, Charley Lampton, and his address, meticulously recorded. Lampton turned abruptly to Armden and swung his arm around to point at him. "What about you? You're old enough to be their father. What are they up to, just between us old-timers, hey?"

Armden looked resentful, and avoided answering by taking a large bite from his Deluxe Iglooburger.

"He's a research physicist, and he's not my father," Napoleon said irritably.

Lampton turned his attention to Napoleon, who quickly snatched his coffee out of the path of the old coot's arm as it swung around like an erratic compass.

"Hey?" Lampton said.

"I said he's not my father," Napoleon repeated.

"Never said he was. Okay, if you're checking mileage, what is it? Hey?"

"24.7 at the last stop," Napoleon answered quickly.

"We hope to do better than that on the way back, on the turnpikes and expressways," Illya added.

"Hey?" said Lampton. They repeated their statements.

Lampton cackled. "You're pretty fast; you work together real well." He suddenly poked a finger at Napoleon's tie clip. Napoleon automatically jumped back, slopping a good portion of the coffee out of his cup.

"Real fast," Lampton said. "Sorry about that. I'll buy you another cup, hey?"

"It's all right; I'm already filled up with coffee."

"Hey?"

Gritting his teeth, Napoleon decided it would be easier to let the old coot buy him a cup. The man trotted off to get it, returned with it before the agents could get away, and planked himself down to watch Napoleon drink it.

Napoleon took a sip to be polite, decided that he really was filled up, and got up to leave.

"Don't waste good coffee," Armden said, picking up the cup and draining it hastily.

They walked around a bit for a final limbering-up before crawling back into the cramped car.

One hour and forty miles later, Napoleon shook his head violently. "Filled up or not, I think I should have drunk the coffee. Do you feel like taking it for awhile?" He glanced at Illya, who shook his head sleepily.

"Better not," Illya said slowly. "I don't know what it is, but I feel too tired to move. Maybe we should stop awhile and try to get a little sleep." Napoleon nodded agreement and started looking for a stopping place. On the outskirts of a small town he spotted a large drive-in and pulled in. As he nosed the car into a parking stall, Illya muttered something sleepily without opening his eyes. Armden was also dozing. After-effects of the drug, Napoleon assumed, since the man had had enough sleep for two or three people in the ordinary course of events. He stifled a yawn as he dropped the car keys into his pocket and walked slowly over to the self-service window just around the corner of the building.

He had just stepped out of sight of the U.N.C.L.E. car when another car pulled into the drive-in and parked a few stalls away. A young man jumped out and walked hurriedly up to the driver's side of the U.N.-C.L.E. car. Without hesitating, he slid into the driver's seat.

"Dr. Armden, Mr. Kuryakin," he said. "You will obey my orders. Both of you get out of this car and go down to the black sedan. Get in it and sit quietly."

There was no response except a muffled snore from Armden. Muttering to himself, the young man shook Illya and Armden awake, then repeated his orders. The sleeping men roused slowly and stumbled out of the car. The young man had to repeat his instructions a third time before they began walking slowly toward the black car. He watched them a minute to make sure they didn't fall asleep on their feet, and then reached for the ignition key. The key was missing, and he swore feelingly, then got back out and crawled into the car head first so he could get at the wiring under the dash. He was still in this undignified position when there was the sound of squealing tires and the slam of several car doors behind him. Seconds later a bearded face was peering at him through the open door on the passenger's side.

"Hey, that's a tough set of wheels. Never saw one quite like it," the face commented enthusiastically.

"Yeah," came another voice, presumably feminine, from behind him. "What kind is it?"

The man looked up hastily and banged his head on

the steering column. "None of your business!" he snapped. "Get out of here; I'm busy."

"Yeah," the feminine voice replied. "We can see. Whatsamatter, you lose your keys?"

"Yes, I lost my keys. Now will you quite bothering me?" He looked toward the rear of the car and saw a big, rectangular box on wheels blocking the U.N.C.L.E. car in completely. "And get that thing out of the way!" he shouted, pointing at the offending object.

"I know how to hot-wire a car," came a polite voice from behind the girl. "I knew a guy who liked to take joy-rides. Anyway, maybe I can help you." A long-haired youth came forward, dropped to his knees and began looking under the dash.

"Wow!" he exclaimed a moment later, "What *is* all this stuff under here?"

The man stood up and looked around. There were a half dozen of the kids around. According to a blazing red and yellow sign on their car, they were the Thundermugs, whatever that meant. One of the new folk-rock outfits, possibly. He swore under his breath, and walked to the front of the car, where he motioned frantically to the black sedan. A hulking man got out from behind the wheel of the sedan and pushed past Illya and Armden.

"Get these kids out of here, Andy," the smaller man hissed as the hulking one approached. "And get that crate out from behind this car."

"Sure, chief." The large man reached down and plucked the hot-wire expert out of the U.N.C.L.E. car, setting him down none too gently on the asphalt.

The bearded youth came forward, protesting. "Hey, we weren't—"

Andy placed a large hand under his chin and shoved, sending the boy staggering back against his own vehicle. Turning, he reached for a girl who had been sitting on the hood of the U.N.C.L.E. car, patting it and saying

"It's cute," to no one in particular. The girl squealed and hopped off the hood on the side opposite Andy.

At this moment, Napoleon came around the corner of the drive-in, carrying a plastic tray loaded with coffee and sandwiches. "Illya! Dr. Armden!" he shouted, dropping the tray. He pulled his gun, and started forward. Illya and Dr. Armden, hearing their names, halted by the side of the black sedan and looked around.

Andy had started to pull his own gun, but the smaller man grabbed him by one arm and headed for the sedan at a run. Napoleon raised his weapon but the kids and then Illya and Dr. Armden were in the line of fire.

The two Thrushes started to force Illya into the car but Napoleon's shouts roused him enough to put up some resistance. The smaller Thrush made a grab for Dr. Armden, but changed his mind as Napoleon approached. He leaped into the sedan instead. His larger companion had already switched on the ignition, and they roared out of the drive-in with squealing tires. Napoleon sent a futile shot after the car as it disappeared down the highway. The Thundermugs, grouped around the U.N.-C.L.E. car, looked on with evident enjoyment.

Napoleon stood staring after the departing sedan for a second, then returned his gun to its shoulder holster, and turned to Illya. "What happened?" he asked.

"He told us to get into his car," Illya said, in a tone implying that this was a perfectly reasonable request. Not having been addressed, Armden stood quietly, his face blank of expression.

Napoleon looked at them, frowning. They looked straight ahead, at nothing in particular.

"Both of you, raise your right hands," Napoleon said sharply.

Illya and Armden raised their hands, without speaking or changing expression.

Napoleon sighed. "Put your arms back down and go back to our car," he instructed. He walked behind them until they climbed into the car. Unclipping his communicator from his pocket, he called Waverly and reported the situation, while the Thundermugs looked on in respectful silence.

Chapter 7

"The Thing To Do Is Work Out A New Questionnaire"

"So," NAPOLEON CONCLUDED his explanation to Sascha Curtis and Rita Berman, "the Harrisburg agents took Illya and Dr. Armden on to New York, and I'm back here looking for a place to stay while I investigate what happened. I wouldn't mind having a place nearby to hide that car, either," he added. "It's a bit conspicuous."

"Amazing, perfectly amazing," Curtis said. "Must be some sort of drug; it couldn't be anything else. Though I don't," he added thoughtfully, "know of any current drug which would produce just that reaction."

"Thrush is quite adept at producing new drugs, if that's what it is," Napoleon replied. "I'm still not certain it isn't some sort of instant hypnotism."

"And the hotel wouldn't give you a room, you say?" Curtis remarked. "I can't think that they're really that full. As far as I know, that hotel has never been filled to capacity."

"Could the hotel manager be a Thrush?" Rita inquired.

"If he was, he'd have made room for me if he had to throw someone else out," Napoleon explained. "Thrush would like nothing better than to have me where they can keep an eye on me. It's more likely that the manager is affected by the same anti-U.N.C.L.E. influence that has struck the rest of the town. That doesn't seem like a drug; one can do wonders with modern drugs, but transferring prejudices seems a bit extraordinary.

"But you had a room in the hotel before," Sascha protested.

"The manager didn't know who we were before," Napoleon said. "He does, now; he was quite hostile about the lack of rooms."

"I know!" Rita exclaimed. "My cousin Lem will rent you a room, and you can keep your car in his barn."

Curtis looked dubious. "Are you sure?" he asked. "Lem Thompson isn't the friendliest soul in the world."

"Oh, he'll do it if I ask him," Rita assured them. "Come on, let's drive out there now, before my next class."

"Wait a minute," Napoleon said. "Who's Lem Thompson, where does he live, and if he lives far enough from town to own a barn, how can I keep the U.N.C.L.E. car hidden and still get back and forth?"

"He's a distant cousin of mine, he has a farm just outside of town, and I can drive you back and forth," Rita explained. "I never knew any real spies before, and I intend to make the most of my opportunity. In a pinch, you could walk there and back, though; it's only a couple of miles from town."

Napoleon finally consented and Rita happily led the way to her car.

Lemuel Thompson was repairing a tractor hitch with a portable welder when Rita arrived in her car, followed by Napoleon in the U.N.C.L.E. vehicle. He shut off the welder and listened, none too patiently, while Rita explained matters.

"Know anything about farming?" he asked Napoleon.

"Nothing," Napoleon said.

"What I thought. Okay, you can stay here, since you're a friend of Rita's. But keep out of my way and don't expect any special attention. I run this place pretty much by myself, and it keeps me too busy to mess with secret agents and public images." He spat contemptuously. "Right now I got to get back to this tractor if I'm going to get my fall plowing done. Rita, you take him in and introduce him to Betsy."

"I see what Professor Curtis meant," Napoleon commented as they walked to the house. "He isn't the friendliest person in the world."

"Oh, Lem is the epitome of the grouch with the heart of gold. It's well buried, but it's there if you dig deep enough. At least he isn't being unfriendly because you're an U.N.C.L.E. agent."

"No, he's just being unfriendly on general principles. I suppose that's an improvement."

They entered the house, where Betsy Thompson, a plump, bustlingly likeable individual, showered them with enough friendliness to make up for her husband's manner. Napoleon was shown to a room, provided with washcloths and towels, and taken on a quick tour of the house, while Betsy and Rita discussed U.N.C.L.E., hypnotism, doctors, Lem's backache, and the lack of rain, Rita's classes, and the latest exploits of Eyre the wombat, whose numerous escapes had apparently made him a local celebrity. Napoleon finally managed to get in a few words to explain that he really should get back to town and do a little investigating.

"And I have to get back to class!" Rita exclaimed, looking at her watch. "If I cut it any more, I'm liable to flunk. It's pretty dull, but I have to make a passing grade, at least."

They started the drive back to town, with Rita humming happily. "Betsy will certainly be happy to have you," she said. "She always enjoys cooking, and Lem usually refuses to eat anything fancier than steak, potatoes, hamburger and apple pie. If he feels exceptionally exotic, he might try a plate of spaghetti. It's one of Betsy's perpetual frustrations; fixing kosher meals for me is about the only fun she gets in the cooking line."

"In that case, let's hope that Illya gets back soon," Napoleon said. "He knows some unusual Russian recipes, and—"

He was interrupted by the beeping of his communicator. Rita glanced sideways as he removed the penlike device from his pocket and spoke into it.

"Solo here."

"Ah, Mr. Solo," came the voice of Waverly. "I trust you're well-rested and alert. You sounded a bit ragged the last time I spoke to you."

"Yes, sir," Napoleon replied. "I got some sleep before driving back here. Have Illya and Dr. Armden arrived safely?"

"Yes, that's the reason I called. We've been running tests on them, and we've discovered significant amounts of an unusual drug in their systems. As yet, we have been unable to identify the compound."

"A drug?" Rita burst in. "Are they all right?"

"I take it you're not alone, Mr. Solo?"

"Mr. Waverly, may I present Rita—what is your last name?"

"Berman."

"Besides being a pretty girl, she's a friend of Professor Curtis and also of U.N.C.L.E. And right now it looks like U.N.C.L.E. needs friends out here." He held the communicator out to her. "Miss Berman, this is Mr. Waverly—and keep your eyes on the road!" he added quickly.

"How did they get you in that little thing, Mr. Waverly?" she asked. "Are you a genie?"

"Not precisely, Miss Berman," Waverly returned, unperturbed. "Although I sometimes suspect that certain of my agents consider me in that light. Now, Mr. Solo, do you have any idea of how Mr. Kuryakin and Dr. Armden could have been given the drug when you weren't?"

Napoleon, who had been staring at Rita to make sure she was joking, jerked his attention back to the communicator. "I can't be sure, sir, but I suspect it might have occurred at our last previous stop. There was a rather obnoxious elderly man there who insisted on joining us while we ate. He had the opportunity to doctor Illya's coffee, and he insisted on buying me a cup which Dr. Armden drank. I kept my own food out of his reach; we considered him merely a nuisance, but I dislike having people wave their hands over my food. How is Illya? Is he still under the influence of the drug?"

"They both seem to be coming out of it, though Dr. Armden appears to be somewhat more susceptible than Mr. Kuryakin. We haven't been able to do much for them, since we haven't identified the drug. Both men appear to be totally without will power; they obey orders without initiative. One more thing which may have a bearing on your problem; both subjects appear to believe implicitly whatever they are told."

Napoleon was silent for a moment before replying. "I suppose we can assume that Armden was given some of the drug last Sunday when we lost him at the airport, and then given orders and turned loose in Midford. It would seem logical to assume that the drug is involved with the rest of the Midford problem."

"I quite agree, Mr. Solo, but there are a number of things which this hypothesis fails to explain."

"I know. There is the problem of administering any drug to an entire population. Until these last incidents, no one seems to have displayed any lack of initiative. So they couldn't have just been fed the drug and ordered to hate U.N.C.L.E. Besides, while Dr. Armden was rational yesterday he didn't remember anything like that. Of course, he didn't recall any other unusual circumstances, either; he seemed completely bewildered by his behavior."

"Yes, Mr. Solo. He is showing signs of the same phenomenon now that he is beginning to throw off the drug's influence again. Both he and Mr. Kuryakin remember the attempted kidnapping yesterday. The affair is indeed a puzzle."

"Miss Berman is driving me to the university to talk with Professor Curtis again. Perhaps he can shed some light on the subject."

"Very well, Mr. Solo. Let me know your findings." The communicator went dead in Waverly's usual abrupt fashion and Napoleon replaced it in his pocket. He looked up as Rita swung the car into the university parking lot. She dashed for her class while Napoleon strolled toward the Liberal Arts building. On the way, he noticed Professor Dodd peering intently into a patch of shrubbery; apparently Eyre was loose again.

"Get settled at Thompson's?" Curtis inquired as he entered.

Napoleon nodded. "I discovered what you meant about him not being friendly, but he agreed to let me stay if I kept out of his way."

Curtis nodded. "That's normal, which is a relief. I shudder to think of Lem Thompson infected with an active dislike of an organization. What's next on your agenda?"

"Seeing you, at the moment. How's the survey coming?"

Curtis's eyes lit up. "Quite well, quite well. It's absolutely amazing. We've covered almost half the families already, and so far . . ." He turned to the desk and burrowed through several stacks of paper. "So far," he continued, "one hundred and eleven families include one or more members who are hostile to U.N.C.L.E. in varying degrees. The amount of hostility varies from pronounced dislike to absolutely white-lipped fury. Frankly, I hadn't realized there were that many people in town who had even heard of U.N.C.L.E."

He laid the paper back on the desk, and looked at Napoleon. "And not a single individual—not one!—can give a rational explanation of his or her feelings!"

"What's their opinion of Thrush?"

"The reactions there are about what I would expect. Most people have never heard of it. A few recognize the name dimly as that of an international organization but are indifferent to it, while about the same number know of its ambition to conquer the world and are opposed to it. Of course there are one or two in favor of its ambition to conquer the world; you get that sort in any opinion poll. Actually, the only anomaly is the anti-U.N.C.L.E. bias, and what seems to be a linked dislike of charities. I confess I don't quite perceive the connection."

"Is there any pattern you can see? Any group, area, occupation, that is more strongly anti-U.N.C.L.E. than the norm?"

"I haven't begun that phase of the survey yet," Curtis explained. "I had intended to wait until all results were in. But if you're impatient . . ." He picked up a stack of papers and riffled through them.

"There's one apparent pattern," he announced finally. "Of course, any snap judgment such as this is subject to verification by a more thorough analysis, you understand. However, I see that almost the entire technical staff of Falco Industries is in the anti-U.N.C.L.E. group."

"That begins to sound like Thrush," Napoleon observed. "Scientists and technicians are their favorite game. That can't account for everyone, though; surely Falco doesn't have that large a technical staff."

Curtis shook his head. "No, and some of these others simply don't fit any pattern that I can see. Perhaps a more detailed analysis will turn up something. But, for example, here's a young man who pumps gas at Joe's Friendly Service. He's not the world's brightest individual; the last noteworthy thing he did was play on the high school basketball team. And here's old Eleazar, the college janitor. Or custodian, as I believe he prefers to be called; he hasn't heard about maintenance engineers yet. I've never heard him discuss anything more intellectual than the latest spy gadget on a TV show. Yet here he is, expressing doubts about international security organizations."

"How about women?" Napoleon asked. "Are they exempt?"

"No, there are a few on the list. Not many, though; not nearly as many as men. However, I would expect that; women are inherently more stable than men."

"Thank you for the kind words," Rita said as she entered. "The class was cancelled today—it would be, just when I'd made a firm resolve to attend—so I came back to pick up pointers on intrigue. Now just reassure me that you meant stable as in personality and not as in horse-stall, and go on with the discussion. I'm all ears."

"Stop identifying with television personalities," Curtis reproved her. She made a face at him.

"I don't think inherent stability has much to do with it," Napoleon said, wrenching the conversation back to its former course.

"Oh?" Curtis looked up from the papers. "Thrush, you mean?"

"More specifically, I meant a new and apparently unknown drug which Thrush seems to have developed."

Curtis looked crestfallen. "I suspected it was too good to be true," he said. Napoleon stared at him. "About the entire town undergoing a psychological change," he explained. "It's really too bad. Although," he looked thoughtful, "I can't quite see how a prejudice could be inculcated by the use of drugs. At the very least there would have to be a command or suggestion accompanying the drug; I suppose a drug that would heighten suggestibility is possible. Are you sure?"

Napoleon shook his head. "At the moment I'm not sure of anything. But since Illya and Armden were pretty obviously drugged with something that made them obey orders, there is a possibility that something similar is being used wholesale in Midford."

Curtis sat on the edge of his desk, lost in thought for a full minute. Optimism gradually returned, and he looked up. "The thing to do is work out a new questionnaire. If the drug is being used on everyone in town we should be able to discover how it's administered. There should be some noticeable side effects."

Napoleon laughed. "You have a way of getting to the heart of the matter," he said. "Mr. Waverly didn't mention side effects that would enable anyone to detect a drug-taker immediately. Once they've voiced anti-U.N.C.L.E. sentiments they're fairly easy. The administration of the drug bothers me; I haven't noticed anyone rushing about madly stabbing people with a hypodermic, or even sprinkling a mysterious powder in everyone's food."

"Maybe the anti-U.N.C.L.E. feeling *is* the side effect," Rita suggested. "Maybe the purpose of the drug is something else altogether."

"It would be a pretty weird side effect," Napoleon answered. "It's hard enough trying to figure out things on the assumption that this is the desired result, without you trying to confuse matters."

"She isn't trying to confuse matters," Curtis said. "She does quite well in that line without trying. According to your story, however, Dr. Armden and your friend Illya acted like zombies after being given the drug yesterday. But Armden and Bennett and the others weren't reacting in that manner when the anti-U.N.C.L.E. feelings were being voiced."

"That's one of the problems," Napoleon admitted. "If it's the same drug, the zombie-state doesn't last."

"Maybe they're conditioned while under the influence

74

of the drug and the conditioning sticks after the drug wears off," Rita offered.

"Doubtful," Napoleon said. "Once the effects of the drug wore off, Armden was perfectly rational on the trip. Besides, the zombie-state lasts at least twenty-four hours. Have you noticed large numbers of glassy-eyed citizenry during the past few months?"

"Maybe they were taken away while the drug was administered," Rita said, unwilling to abandon her best idea.

"You might add a question about trips to our next survey," Napoleon said, "but I doubt if it will prove anything. Another problem is the non-scientists on the list. I can see Thrush trying to brainwash the Falco staff or the instructors here at the university. But janitors and gas station attendants? No."

"To divert suspicion!" Rita exclaimed.

"You don't give up easily, do you?" Napoleon asked. "Well, it's worth looking into; at this point almost anything is worth looking into. Assuming that it really is a drug, the major problem is to find out how it's administered."

"How did Illya get his?" Rita asked.

"Probably in his coffee."

"There you are! Easiest thing in the world to drop a pill in someone's coffee, then say 'Come with me' and that's it." She leaned back triumphantly.

"Except that this sort of thing would be noticed, eventually," Napoleon pointed out. "Remember, this is being used on an entire community."

"The water supply," Curtis suggested. "No, Eleazar got it, and he never touches drinking water—or any other kind, if he can help it."

"How about restaurants?" Rita asked. "There aren't many eating places in town; find out which one is patronized by the victims."

Napoleon frowned thoughtfully. "That gives me an

idea. Could you drop the survey for a day and put your students on another job?"

"Easiest thing in the world; as long as it gets them out of class, they won't care. What do you have in mind?"

"Have your students collect samples of water, food, drinks, everything they can lay their hands on. I'll need samples, carefully labelled, from all over town. Label should include nature of sample, place collected, and if possible the name of the distributor, trucking company or whatever. I'll send them to New York and have them analyzed."

"I see," Curtis said. "Very well, I'll put them on the job tomorrow. Rita, could you get instruction sheets mimeographed?"

The girl nodded. "And what will you be doing while everyone else is doing your work?" she asked Napoleon.

"Studying effective leadership," he replied. "In addition, I'll do some work on Professor Curtis' survey and see if I can work out a pattern. Then I'd like a file of back issues of the local newspaper, and if possible a history of Midford. Would the university library have those?"

"Certainly," Curtis said. "Rita, show him the library. You can do your research right there; I'll be along after my next class. I'll bring a bottle of my new rose hip extract; I just made the first batch of the season."

A few students gave Napoleon and Rita curious stares as they walked across the campus, and Rita laughed delightedly. "I'll have something to crow over, now," she explained. "Being escorted by a real live spy, no less. Wait until I get a chance to tell this to Flavia!"

Napoleon looked at her inquiringly, and she explained. "My best friend, locally: Flavia Whateley. She lives in this mouldering mansion on the other side of town, and she has all these stories about the odd sort of people her father associates with. But I'll bet she's never seen a real secret agent!"

Napoleon smiled, then stiffened slightly. "Don't make your interest obvious, but take a look at the man in the gray suit walking on the opposite side of the street and see if you know him."

Rita looked. "Yes, I know him. He's Jules Adams, president of one of the local finance companies. Why?"

"Because the last time I saw him, he was whipping up the mob at the Fort Wayne airport. In a way, it's a relief; if the anti-U.N.C.L.E. feeling is restricted to Midford it will be easier to combat than if it is more widespread. Of course, his being in the mob could be coincidence, but I doubt it. I thought it formed and broke up much too rapidly for it to be genuine. Thrush harassment is something we're used to."

"It also means," Rita commented, "that Thrush is attempting to divert suspicion from Midford—and probably from other things as well," she added, smugly.

Chapter 8

"A Powerful Figure Of Evil Indeed"

NAPOLEON FOUND HIMSELF becoming fascinated with some of the folklore of Midford. Unfortunately, the history had been written on the occasion of the town's centennial in 1937, and had never been updated.

Some of the more interesting historical characters seemed to belong to the Whateley family. Napoleon wondered if Rita's friend was a relative. According to the history, one Jabez Whateley, together with his wife and son, had migrated to Midford from Salem, Massachusetts just after the turn of the century. He had built a duplicate of the original Whateley mansion; a

somewhat bizarre structure, according to the description
given. Apparently the elder Whateley's refusal to become
neighborly had roused the resentment of local citizens;
before long there were rumors, faithfully set down in
the history, that the Whateleys were devil-worshippers
and worse. Midford residents hurrying past the Whateley house after dark had reported strange sights and
sounds. The death or disappearance of any farm animal
for miles around was instantly attributed to Jabez
Whateley's evil influence.

Neighborhood fear had culminated one night when
the daughter of Whateley's nearest neighbor failed to
show up for supper. A mob had formed, ready to storm
the Whateley mansion, but it had been broken up by
the prompt and firm action of the sheriff and a hastily
assembled lot of deputies. The next day the distraught
parents had received a telephone call from the missing girl, announcing that she had eloped with the mini-
ster's son. Predictably, the reaction of the local populace was a baffled rage at being balked. Whateley's
reputation remained sinister until he died, whereupon
his son, Jabez Junior, had inherited the hostility along
with the mansion.

Napoleon considered the story thoughtfully before
delving into the file of newspapers. Active dislike of
strangers in Midford was evidently an ancient and
honorable tradition. Could Thrush have somehow persuaded Midford residents that U.N.C.L.E. was connected with the iniquitous Whateley family? It might be
wise to interview the current Jabez Whateley.

The file of newspapers proved little more help than
the history. Napoleon was amused to note· that the
paper, after beginning life as *The Midford Press,* had
changed its title to *The Midford Paper.* "Everyone," the
editor explained, "calls it 'the Midford paper,' so why
not name it that?"

The only really interesting fact Napoleon discovered

was that Jabez Whateley had recently built a small television station to serve Midford and the surrounding area. The area in question was one of freak reception in which only the most elaborate antenna array could pick up the network-affiliated stations in South Bend, Fort Wayne, and Indianapolis. Whateley's transmitter in Bippus was received with loud public acclaim. Residents may not have become fully reconciled to Whateley, but they apparently refrained from making their feelings public. Snide comments in the newspaper had ceased after station WHPL-TV went on the air.

Napoleon looked up from the desk as the office door opened and Sascha Curtis staggered in with a huge cardboard box in his arms. He put the box down and dropped onto a convenient couch.

"Some of your samples," he explained. "There are ten more like it in my classroom; they're beginning to get in the way when I conduct classes."

Napoleon frowned. "You're sure you have the correct definition of sample? We aren't stocking up against atomic attack, you know."

Curtis reached into the box and pulled out a jar of strawberry preserves. "We could hardly ask the proprietor to spread some on a cracker for us. Do you have any idea of the variety of goods stocked by the average grocery store? We haven't even started on the restaurants."

"Mr. Waverly isn't going to be at all happy with the cost of flying this stuff to New York. Couldn't you extract a small sample from each can or jar and put it in a collecting bottle or test tube or something?"

"We need all those for our samples from the restaurants, vending machines, water supply, and so on. Even if we could get more test tubes and collecting bottles, they aren't the cheapest products in the world. Incidentally, I assume I'll be reimbursed for the cost of all this stuff?"

Napoleon winced. "Yes, we'll pay you for them, even if the cost comes out of my salary—and it might. Could I further impose on you to the extent of borrowing a car to get all this stuff to the airport when it's packed?"

Before Curtis could answer, Napoleon's communicator warbled from his coat pocket. "Solo here," he said.

"Ah, Mr. Solo," said Waverly. "Mr. Kuryakin will be back with you shortly. He seems fully recovered from the drug. We've arranged for him to arrive in Fort Wayne on the 9:30 flight this evening. Dr. Armden has been a little slower to recover, but he's improving. He and his wife are being suitably guarded, of course."

"Could you also make arrangements to have ten . . ." Napoleon paused as Curtis shook his head violently and held up three fingers. "Thirteen?" Curtis nodded. "Thirteen cases of food and drink samples flown to New York?"

"Thirteen cases, Mr. Solo? You said you were obtaining samples, not . . ."

"Not storing up against atomic attack," Napoleon finished for him. "I know, sir, but do you realize the variety of goods stocked by the average grocery store? We had to be thorough."

"Of course, Mr. Solo, but thirteen cases!"

"Also," Napoleon added, "there is the matter of reimbursing Professor Curtis for his purchase of the sample and the various test tubes and collecting bottles used to transport some of them."

Mr. Waverly sighed. "I suppose it can't be helped. The battle against the forces of evil must never flag for lack of finances. Heaven knows I've had sufficient practice in justifying your expenditures before the Board of Directors; I should be able to explain this one, too." He sounded somewhat doubtful.

"Thank you, sir. We should have the samples packed in time to take them to the airport when we meet Illya."

"Very well, Mr. Solo. I'll make the proper arrangements here." The communicator went dead.

Illya stared at the car, which towered above the others in the airport parking lot, giving him the impression that he could have driven the U.N.C.L.E. car underneath it without touching anything.

"It's a Checker," Rita explained. She climbed into the driver's seat with Napoleon on her right. Illya got into the back and wandered about for a short time before sitting down.

"Where's the meter?" he inquired.

"You're too late," Napoleon told him. "I said the same thing the first time I rode in it."

"I know agents start to think alike when they've been together long enough," Illya complained. "But I had hoped for a better fate. Do we have time to stop at a restaurant? I didn't eat at all while I was drugged and I have some catching up to do. The meal on the plane was just an appetizer."

"If you'll wait until we get back to Midford," Napoleon said encouragingly, "Professor Curtis has prepared a delicious watercress salad."

Rita laughed as she swung the car onto the highway. "I know a good place here; I guess I can ignore my diet for once."

A few minutes later, the three were seated at a well-lit table and Napoleon was filling Illya in on his recent activity.

"I want to talk to Whateley," he concluded. "Logically, there's no connection between the Whateley family and U.N.C.L.E. But sometimes logical explanations fail to satisfy me."

Rita had listened with interest; now she spoke. "I can take you to see Jabez; didn't know you were interested. He's an odd sort, but his daughter Flavia will be delighted. I've been telling her about you. I did tell you that she's a friend?"

Napoleon nodded.

"I'd planned to go out there tomorrow anyway," Rita continued. "There's a Hallowe'en festival coming up that we're both working on; you two can come along and quiz Jabez." She laughed. "I'll be interested to know what sort of answers you get."

Illya had been quietly thoughtful since Napoleon had mentioned the Whateley television station. Now he spoke slowly. "I had time to think while I was recovering. Once the drug began to wear off my mind was clear, but I just didn't have any urge to communicate. Then before I left New York I talked with some of the communications experts in Section Four. Napoleon, what do you think of subliminal suggestions to explain all this? I couldn't think how they would be delivered, but with only one TV station in the area, it wouldn't be too hard to arrange. I'd been thinking of movies, but I don't know what percentage of the populace attends movies regularly. TV simplifies matters."

Napoleon frowned. "I thought they had proved that subliminal advertising wasn't particularly effective."

"By itself, no; but don't forget the effects of the drug. A combination of the two could explain things pretty well."

Napoleon was studying the idea when Rita reached over and tapped his arm. "If you want to meet Jabez Whateley," she informed him, "he just walked in the door." Without waiting for an answer, she began waving frantically at an erect, white-haired man wearing a black suit and an opera cape. He spotted Rita and his cadaverous features readjusted themselves into a wintry smile as he approached their table.

"Miss Berman," he said, bowing slightly. "How pleasant to see you." The voice was deep, with careful enunciation and a tone that had a sepulchral quality. It was, Napoleon decided, an ominous voice; one which did not match the innocuous topics of conversation. Whateley answered questions about his daughter and mentioned that parts of the forthcoming Hallowe'en pageant would be shown on his television station.

"What better way to enhance the Whateley reputation?" he said with a sinister chuckle.

Rita almost forgot to introduce the two agents. Whateley bowed formally to the men.

"I've heard of your organization," he said quietly. "A veritable bulwark against the forces of evil." The sinister chuckle came again. "Or at least, against the forces of earthly evil."

Napoleon glanced at Rita, who was busily suppressing a giggle. "I'm afraid earthly evil keeps us busy enough at present," he replied. "One thing at a time, and all that."

"I doubt that Mr. Waverly would approve any budgetary items for the suppression of supernatural evil," Illya commented. "Though considering his penchant for insisting that all flights be made by coach, I suppose he might be willing to look into the matter of broomsticks."

"Of course, gentlemen," Whateley said. "No one believes in evil that they can't see. If it doesn't come neatly packaged and labeled, as in the case of your rival, Thrush, everyone tends to ignore it. It's very difficult to combat something that one is ignoring." He chuckled again.

Napoleon watched Whateley closely while keeping a pleasant smile on his face. "I understand your father had just the opposite problem. People believed in an evil that didn't exist, and were willing to lynch him for it."

Whateley shrugged skeletally. "People were more ready to believe in things of the spirit fifty years ago," he said. "Not to mention that father contributed heavily to his own legend; he was positively delighted at the opportunity to appear exotically evil. I'm afraid that I seem to have inherited the tendency." He swirled his cape dramatically.

Napoleon smiled understandingly.

"Of course," Whateley continued, eyeing the U.N.-C.L.E. agents speculatively, "there is always the possibility that the local residents were right. The old gods were not a benevolent sort. A man who could invoke their aid would be a powerful figure of evil indeed."

"Old gods?" Napoleon inquired.

"Yes, Mr. Solo. There were gods before Jehovah, and humanity did not always give even lip-service to the current ideals of brotherhood and tolerance. What does a god who has lost his worshippers do, Mr. Solo? He can no longer act, but, being immortal, he cannot die, either. He exists in a formless limbo. There are gods waiting there, Mr. Solo; beings so powerful, and so evil, that all mankind might not withstand them if they returned."

Napoleon nodded noncommittally. "I have a feeling," he said, "that the people of Midford would be willing to believe in the old gods. They are certainly willing enough to believe that U.N.C.L.E. is in league with the devil."

Whateley looked interested. "That seems unusual. You're generally regarded as being on the, ah, other side, aren't you? Certainly you don't appear very diabolical. Why would anyone consider you evil?"

"We haven't found a reason," Napoleon said. "That's why I wanted to talk to you. As the object of a hate campaign of your own, I thought you might be able to shed some light on the subject."

Whateley shook his head. "I'm afraid not; the reason for the dislike of the Whateleys is all too plain. Is this U.N.C.L.E. phobia a recent phenomenon?"

"Apparently. In fact, we're beginning to suspect that it's not natural; that a drug of some kind may be involved."

Whateley chuckled again, and Illya involuntarily shivered. "Or perhaps an evil spell, Mr. Solo? An enchantment? I didn't realize that secret agents were so sensitive about their images."

Napoleon looked hurt. "Unlike some organizations," he explained, "we occasionally must depend on public good will. But whatever the problem is, we'll manage to get it solved." He attempted to look confident and succeeded in appearing slightly fatuous.

"You mean that both of you are in Midford simply to find out why people don't like U.N.C.L.E.? I should think there would be more serious calls on your time. I suppose I could sell you some advertising time on my TV station and you could get a good public relations firm to handle the case. That sort of thing does wonders for General Motors, I understand."

"I'm afraid our budget would never stand for it." Napoleon sighed dramatically. "We sometimes have trouble when our hotel bill lists an extra for a TV set in the room; if we can't afford to watch it, I'm sure we could never afford to buy time on it."

"That shouldn't bother you in Midford," Whateley suggested. "The facilities of the local hotel are not the most up-to-date."

"We aren't staying at the hotel, though," Napoleon said. "The manager is one of the townspeople who dislikes U.N.C.L.E. Currently we're staying with Rita's cousin, but . . ." He let his voice trail off.

"That's an inconvenient base of operations," Whateley said. "It's really quite distant from Midford." He paused thoughtfully. "Why don't you accept my hospitality? I have a fine house not too far from town; there's just Flavia and myself and a small domestic staff. With a few lovely exceptions," he bowed toward Rita, "we don't have visitors. I'm afraid the Whateleys are still not considered a part of the community."

Napoleon studied the offer. "It might be best, if we wouldn't disturb you."

"Not at all, not at all." Whateley smiled, and Napoleon discovered that his smile could be as sinister as his chuckle. "I'm sure Miss Berman can vouch for my character, if you have any lingering doubts."

Rita nodded agreeably. "You'll like it there. If you want to look up any more local history, I'm sure the Whateley library contains at least as many volumes as the university library; perhaps more."

Whateley smiled in what might be construed as delight. "Are you fellow bibliophiles? Delightful. I do have a quite extensive and, er, unusual library. You must avail yourselves of it."

"Very well," Napoleon agreed. "What time tomorrow should we arrive?"

"It's still early," Whateley responded, pulling a huge gold watch from a vest pocket and glancing at it. "You could easily come back with me as soon as we've finished the meal."

Napoleon shook his head. "I don't think we should. I'm afraid Mr. Thompson might be somewhat annoyed by all the packing and moving at this late hour. He's been very considerate, and I wouldn't want to disturb him."

"I see," said Whateley. "Having met Lem Thompson, I can well understand. Tomorrow, then; any time that suits your convenience. You come, too," he said, turning to Rita. "Flavia wanted to ask you something about costumes for the pageant."

Rita nodded, and Whateley stalked away from the table, paused momentarily at the door to whirl his cape about his shoulders in a theatrical gesture, and departed into the night.

"He forgot to get anything to eat," Illya commented.

"True," Napoleon agreed. "I think he was too interested in maneuvering us into accepting his invitation to stay with him."

"Perhaps," said Illya. "But you were working just as hard to maneuver him into issuing the invitation, and it didn't spoil your appetite."

"You noticed, did you? Well, it takes a devious mind to know one. I'd like to be able to keep an eye on Jabez Whateley. Your idea of subliminal suggestions, his new TV station and his showing up here so conveniently: it all strikes me as a pretty healthy coincidence."

Illya nodded. "If he isn't involved, his place sounds like a good base. If he is, then it will be easier to keep an eye on him while he thinks he's keeping an eye on us. Of course, he isn't stupid. We suspect him, but he knows that we suspect him, and since we know that he knows . . ."

"Never mind," Napoleon said as he rose and picked up the check. "You know, we really are beginning to think alike."

"Incidentally, how many hours a day does Whateley's television station broadcast?" Napoleon asked as Rita swung the car into Lem Thompson's driveway.

"About twelve, I think," she replied.

"What time does it go off the air?"

Rita shrugged. "That depends on what part of the country you live in. Here in Midford, it goes off at midnight."

Illya looked baffled. "It broadcasts to different areas at different times?"

"Not really," Rita explained. "It's just that part of the area is on Eastern Standard time, and part of it is on Central Standard. Then there's one section on Central Daylight, but that's the same as Eastern Standard. I think." She paused and frowned thoughtfully. "Over by Hunterton you get into Eastern Daylight in the summer, but I think they've switched back to Eastern Standard now. Then a few farmers still set their clocks on Sun Time, which is a half hour faster than Central Standard. Or is it a half hour slower?" She paused again.

Napoleon blinked. "It seems awfully confusing."

"Very. But it has its advantages. One of the more enterprising students at the university has been making good money by selling mimeographed copies of his conversion table. So people in Midford can tell when the stores will close in Bippus and vice versa."

"But I thought time zones had been standardized by law," Illya said.

"Oh, they have," Rita said casually. "But can you see someone standardizing Lem Thompson? This state has been arguing over the standard time zones for the past five years, and they're no closer to an agreement now than they were when they started."

"I see your point," Napoleon admitted. "Where is this TV station, anyway? The newspaper just said Bippus."

"You can't miss it," Rita informed them with the cheery confidence of someone who has never tried to follow directions. "It's right downtown, across from the hotel. Why? Are you going to raid it?" Eagerness for adventure was apparent in her voice.

"Eventually," said Napoleon. "But not until we have something a little more definite to go on."

"Yes," Illya added helpfully. "We're having enough image problems now; imagine what would happen if we were caught burglarizing an innocent TV station."

Rita looked unconvinced, but failed to pursue the subject as the agents got out of the car. With a wave, she drove off, and the looming hulk of the Checker disappeared into the darkness.

"Well, let's go," Napoleon said.

"Aren't you the mad, impetuous boy, though," said Illya.

Napoleon shrugged. "If you'd prefer to wait until Rita thinks of a good excuse to come along . . ."

They walked to the U.N.C.L.E. car.

Chapter 9

"If I Didn't Know Better, I'd Say This Was A Chain"

THE OFFICES OF WHPL-TV occupied the second floor
over the Gackenheimer Feed Store. Napoleon and Illya
strolled by the front of the building, trying to look as
though they had legitimate business on the totally deserted street at two o'clock in the morning. Napoleon
halted to inspect a sign advertising Candied Baby Pig
Pusher. "I'd think it would be hard to get hooked on
candied baby pigs," he commented. "Though I've heard
that chocolate covered ants are considered a delicacy
in some circles."

Illya grimaced and urged Napoleon along to the alley
next to the building. The agents disappeared into it.

"I wonder if they'll have a watchman?" Illya asked.

"A possibility, if Thrush is involved," said Napoleon.
"I don't think they're expecting us, though. Having a
watchman tends to make people wonder what sort of
valuables need to be watched. We might be lucky. This
stairway seems to be what we're looking for. You keep
a lookout down here while I see about the door."

The door at the top of the stairs was, of course,
locked. As quiet as the town was, blowing the lock

90

would attract too much unwanted attention. After studying the lock by the light of his small flashlight, Napoleon extracted a piece of thin wire from a coat pocket and inserted it in the keyhole. After some experimental poking he pulled the wire back out, bent it to shape, and reinserted it. Some experimental twists revealed the need for further modifications. The next trial produced the satisfying sound of the bolt being withdrawn. He gestured to Illya, who quickly joined him.

"I'm going inside," Napoleon said. "You stay here. If I run into trouble, I'll make enough noise for you to hear and come bail me out. If someone starts investigating from outside, you make enough noise to warn me."

"You didn't say anything about bailing me out," Illya complained.

"Anyone you run into is likely to be an officer of the law, in which case I'll bail you out in the morning. Just pretend you're a burglar and keep U.N.C.L.E.'s image untarnished."

Illya nodded unhappily and tried to look like a burglar. Napoleon switched on his light and moved into the studio.

The place was about what he had expected: some offices, an art department for local advertising, a couple of small sound stages for live programming, a film library. Making his way into the library, he found the films neatly racked and a portable viewer for examining film strips set up on a table. *If Thrush is involved,* he thought, *they're going out of their way to be helpful.*

On inspection, the majority of the films turned out to be commercials. They were filed by sponsor name; a thorough search failed to reveal the cross-index by program that he expected. Not that it made much difference. Professor Curtis had mentioned a local news broadcast that almost everyone watched, but subliminal messages were as likely to appear in one film as another.

He began selecting films at random and running them through the viewer.

To his surprise, he found subliminal messages in the first film, and the second, and the third. It began to look as though every advertising film in the room had been tampered with by Thrush. Additional single frames had been spliced into the films, so that each would be shown just long enough for the viewer's subconscious to pick up the message. Most of the messages were just two words, such as "U.N.C.L.E. Communist," or "U.N.C.L.E. Killers." Others simply had the U.N.C.L.E name overlayed across photos of gangsters, hooded executioners, and the like.

He found a few frames that showed skid row bums, panhandling in one frame, mugging someone in another, and some which seemed to portray Thrush's favorite axiom, "Might is Right." The Thrush name was never mentioned, but it seemed obvious that they were the originators of the messages. Apparently in addition to castigating U.N.C.L.E., they were attempting to implant a general attitude which would make the citizens more receptive to Thrush domination in the name of strong, efficient government. There might be other films implicating Thrust directly, but he had found what he suspected. It wouldn't do to jeopardize a successful mission by making protracted examinations of all the films in stock.

He carefully replaced the films where he had found them, made sure the viewer was in its original position, and rejoined Illya at the back door. After locking the door behind them, they returned to their car and, as they drove back to Lem Thompson's farm, they reported their success to Waverly.

The warbling of his communicator awakened Napoleon the next morning. He groped around on the table next to the bed and eventually located the device.

"Solo here," he mumbled.

"Good morning, Mr. Solo," came the precise voice of Waverly. Napoleon shook his head and untangled himself from the covers enough to sit up.

"The analysis of the food and drink samples you sent us has been completed," Waverly continued. "With most interesting results."

"So soon?" The efficiency of the U.N.C.L.E. lab technicians never ceased to amaze Napoleon.

"Yes, Mr. Solo, and a pretty penny of overtime it cost us, too. But I'm happy to say it was not spent in vain. The drug found previously in Mr. Kuryakin and Dr. Armden was present in every sample of liquid from Midford vending machines."

"Were those the only positive samples?" Napoleon asked.

"The only ones, Mr. Solo. Do you know who services the vending machines in Midford?"

"No sir, but it shouldn't be difficult to find out. Actually, vending machines explain many of our problems, including the big one of why there was no pattern as to who was affected. We didn't think to include a question on whether or not the individual patronized vending machines. And they would be ideal for conversion of almost everyone in a big industrial plant like Falco."

"Umm, yes," Waverly agreed. "But it does not explain what Thrush is planning. It seems an unlikely way for them to raise an army to do battle with U.N.C.L.E., especially since we have found no similar situations anywhere else in the world."

Napoleon reluctantly agreed. "But we may know more once we've located the vending machine company. I'd be willing to bet that Jabez Whateley has a hand in it somewhere."

"I don't recall that name, Mr. Solo."

Napoleon explained their meeting with Whateley.

"Incidentally," he added, "I think it would be a good idea to provide Illya with more freedom of action. There is no need for both of us to remain under Whateley's eye. After we have moved, I'll report to you. When I do, you order Illya back to New York. I'll make sure Whateley is listening. Then Illya can go back to Thompson's, away from prying eyes. The limelight will be focused on me, and Illya will be free to skulk about and run down any leads I uncover."

"Very well, Mr. Solo. I will await your call."

As Napoleon turned the car into the long driveway leading to Jabez Whateley's home, he decided that Rita's use of the term "mansion" had not been an exaggeration. The house was a huge, rambling affair. The gravel drive curved around the front yard, with an extension at one side leading to an oversized garage in the rear. A few outbuildings were visible beyond. House and garage were covered with ivy; a fence, sagging under a load of the same vines, straggled off at one side of the yard. Napoleon started to apply the brakes in front of the house, but the skeletal form of Whateley appeared and motioned for him to bring the car back to the garage.

"Glad you could make it, gentlemen," Whateley said as the agents got out of the car. "You're just in time for what is called supper in these latitudes. I'm sure you will appreciate a simple, nourishing meal after a long day of agenting." He smiled in his usual sinister fashion and motioned them to a door. It opened on a broad hallway that apparently ran the length of the house.

Wateley led them to an enormous living room, dominated by a huge fireplace. Napoleon's eye was caught by the picturesque but morbid paintings adorning the walls. A reproduction of Bosch's "Garden of Delights" hung over the fireplace, and he noted works by Hogarth, Dore, Klee, and Prosser. Whateley noticed his gaze and brought forth his sinister chuckle.

"I find they lend a homey touch and a certain individuality all too often lacking in most modern homes," he said. "Just make yourselves at home while I check on Casimir. He's a good cook, but he does need prodding." With that, he disappeared down the hall, leaving the agents on their own.

After a few minutes inspecting the paintings, both agents began wandering idly about. Just off the living room, they came upon a large entrance foyer with a wide marble staircase leading to the second floor. Something on the staircase caught Napoleon's eye; he walked over to peer through the balustrade. When Illya joined him a moment later, he was curiously inspecting a long length of log chain lying on the stairs. He picked up a section and held it up for Illya's inspection.

"If I didn't know better, I'd say this was a chain," he observed.

"Remarkable deduction," Illya returned. "Rather strange placement, wouldn't you say?"

"Conspicuous to say the least," Napoleon agreed, looking past Illya toward the front door, only a few feet from the bottom of the stairs. "I suppose it's possible that Whateley is addicted to orgies and human sacrifice in the dark of the moon."

They were still speculating when Whateley reappeared a minute later. He saw the chain and sighed.

"That girl! I've told her a thousand times not to leave her things lying around the house." Whateley turned to what looked like a stuffed vulture on the mantel above the fireplace. "Flay!" he bellowed into the bird's beak.

"Yes, Father?" came a feminine voice, apparently from an ornamental tapestry depicting the Salem witch trials.

"We have guests," Whateley said to the vulture, "and you've been littering the stairway again. Come up here to meet the guests and remove your chain."

"Yes, Father," the tapestry replied obediently.

Whateley turned to the agents. "Never could locate anybody around this place until I put in an intercom system. You'll have to excuse my daughter; she's a good girl, but occasionally a trifle untidy about her hobby."

He led them back to the living room and motioned to a pair of overstuffed chairs. As they waited for Whateley's daughter to appear, Napoleon had time to consider the sort of hobby which would make use of a thirty-foot chain and be appropriate to the Whateley mansion, while Illya speculated on what the chairs might have been stuffed with. Both agents shuddered inwardly but maintained calm exteriors.

Flavia might well have been a lovely girl, but it was hard to tell. She appeared in army fatigues and an old sweatshirt, with her long black hair tied up in a ragged scarf. She came over to the agents without waiting for an introduction.

"You must be the two U.N.C.L.E. agents that Rita is so excited about," she said, extending a hand. "And I can see why," she added.

"Flavia," her father interrupted. "Don't forget your chain."

"I'm sorry, Father," she said. "I was going to take it down to the basement but the phone rang and I forgot." She hoisted the chain and formed it into a coil as she spoke. Napoleon sprang forward with an offer to help.

"Oh, no," she declined. "It's all part of the job."

Napoleon and Illya looked blank.

"Didn't Father tell you? I do metal sculpture. Would you like to see some of it after supper?" She paused, the chain looped over her shoulder, and looked closely at the agents. "In fact, would you have time to pose for me? I just got in some new bronze castings. You in particular, Mr. Kuryakin, have the look of a refined savage that would go well in bronze."

Illya smiled graciously. "I'm sure the spirit of Mr.

Solo could be caught more completely in brass, if you have any available," he said pleasantly.

Flavia looked a trifle uncertain as she shifted the chain and edged toward the stairs. "You must excuse me, though. I have some iron rods heating and I must get back and shape them while they're at the right temperature." She clanked down the stairs.

"Now, gentlemen," Whateley said, "I'll show you to your rooms."

Napoleon nodded, then snapped his fingers as if he had suddenly remembered something. "We haven't informed New York that we've moved yet," he said. "If you'll excuse me a moment . . ." He pulled out his communicator.

Waverly answered promptly, accepted Napoleon's report with bland unconcern, and requested that Illya return to New York that evening. Illya turned to Whateley.

"It appears I must eat and run," he said. "I'm sorry to appear so ungracious."

Napoleon watched Whateley closely as their new host assured Illya that he understood perfectly, and that Illya was welcome to return at any time. Whateley's expression was, as always, somewhat unpleasant and a trifle frightening, but it was not at all informative.

Chapter 10

"You're Developing A Very Creditable Mean Streak"

DINNER WAS SUPERB. Napoleon decided that the food alone would have been ample justification for moving into the Whateley mansion. After the rash of drive-ins, anything would have looked good; but a menu that included *pieczen barania a la sarna, pierogi z kapusta, mizeria,* and *dasza jaglana,* all topped off with *babka zrumem,* was enough to send Napoleon's palate into a spasm of ecstasy. Even Illya, normally as taciturn about food as about most other subjects, was delighted. The Kuryakins, he said, had been fond of Polish food ever since a distant ancestor had been a member of the Russian occupation forces in 1795. Napoleon only raised his eyebrows at the information, but Casimir poked his head through the swinging doors long enough to glare briefly at Illya, then withdrew to his kitchen.

After the meal, Napoleon strolled with apparent aimlessness around the house and Illya returned to the library. Entering the huge, booklined room some time later, Napoleon found him engrossed in a large leatherbound tome, the name of which seemed to have been worn away through years of use.

"Time to get you to the airport," Napoleon announced, for the benefit of anyone who might be listening.

Illya looked up. "I hadn't realized it was so late," he said. "Alhazred is a particularly fascinating writer." He rose, returned the book to the crowded shelves, and followed Napoleon into the hall.

Jabez had apparently withdrawn to some other part of the huge house but Flavia met them at the door, wearing a black sheath dress that caught and held Napoleon's interest.

"No sculpting tonight?" he inquired.

"No. The drama group is meeting to plan the Hallowe'en program."

"That would seem to be more in your father's line," Napoleon remarked.

Flavia laughed, a little uncertainly, Napoleon thought. "He does offer suggestions now and then, but they tend to make the rest of the group a little nervous. In fact, they occasionally make me that way, and I *know* he's only joking. Rita is the only person I know who enjoys his sense of humor entirely."

"Yes, he does put up an effective front," Napoleon

admitted, then glanced at his wrist watch. "But we really must be going if we're going to make the airport in time." The two agents bowed slightly and walked across to the U.N.C.L.E. car. After the few seconds it took to fit themselves in, it purred away from the Whateley mansion.

After driving ostentatiously through Midford on the highway to Fort Wayne, they waited until they were out of sight of the town and then swung onto a side road. Some minutes and several turns later, they emerged on another highway, about a hundred yards from a Bippus city limits sign. Just beyond the sign, they passed a large, ramshackle building with the words "Bippus Vending Service" barely visible in the chipped paint over the front door.

"Bullseye the first try," Illya murmured as Napoleon drove past the building about fifty yards to another side road. "Amazing."

Napoleon doused the lights and pulled the car well off the side of the road. They were hidden from the building by some trees and a rise in the ground. Despite the fact that they were officially within the city limits, there were no other buildings or houses in sight.

"It doesn't look like the sort of place that would be worth guarding," Napoleon said. "But I don't suppose everything can be as easy as the TV station was, particularly if they're on their guard now."

Illya nodded his agreement. "One of us had better check it out and dispose of any watchman. The other can stay with the car until the coast is clear."

"Eminently logical," Napoleon agreed. "I'll bring the car around behind the building as soon as you give me an all-clear signal."

Illya glanced at Napoleon, comfortably ensconced behind the wheel. "Okay, I owe you a favor from last Tuesday. You can sit here in safety while I dispose of Thrush's minion or minions. I skulk better than you do, anyway." He opened the weapons compartment and pulled out the Mercox.

"That seems rather drastic for quietly subduing a guard," Napoleon observed. "As I recall, it made a good anti-aircraft gun not long ago."

"It's a very versatile device," Illya assured him as he reached down for a handful of projectiles. "These, for instance, are hypodermic darts. They were originally developed for animal control, but a few modifications in the U.N.C.L.E. labs have made them suitable for Thrush control. And these," he reached for another handful, "are tear gas. And I'll take a couple of the explosive loads just in case there's a safe or something our normal burgling tools won't handle." Stuffing the projectiles into his pockets and carefully stowing the long-barrelled pistol inside his jacket, he climbed out of the car and started up the wooded hill that separated them from the Bippus Vending Service.

It took only a few minutes for Illya to top the hill and dodge through the trees and bushes until he stood behind a small tree a few yards from the building itself. The place looked deserted. An old truck stood in the driveway behind it, and the weed-grown yard was littered with broken bottles and odd pieces of rusting machinery.

Illya remained behind the tree for several minutes, observing the building closely. Nothing stirred, and only one window showed light. Waiting until there were no cars on the highway, he slipped across the yard and examined the back door. Surprisingly, it yielded to a few turns of his picklock. Holding the Mercox in readiness, he eased the door open a crack and slithered inside.

Closing the door quietly, he stood where he was for a moment to accustom his eyes to the blackness inside the building. The night light he had seen from the outside was apparently in a front office at the other end of the building. He cautiously felt his way forward. He had reached a workbench which blocked his way and was starting to move along it when he heard the sound of footsteps. He froze, shading his eyes with one hand and bringing up the gun with the other.

A door across the room opened and a figure was momentarily outlined against the light in the background. The door shut and a flashlight beam swept across the floor.

Illya aimed as carefully as he could in the blackness for a point just above and to the right of the flashlight. He squeezed the trigger. The report was alarmingly loud in the confined quarters and was followed by a sharp exclamation from behind the flashlight. The light swung up to shine on Illya for an instant, then wavered and dropped. There was the sound of a falling body and the clatter of the flashlight as it hit the concrete floor and went out.

Ears straining for any sound, Illya waited in complete silence for a full minute before taking his own flashlight and making his way across the room. Using the watchman's own belt, Illya tied him securely to one leg of a sturdy looking workbench. Satisfied that even if the man did wake up before he was supposed to, he could do no damage, Illya searched him and removed a Thrush communicator and a revolver from his pockets. With his own communicator, Illya called Napoleon in.

By the time Napoleon had parked the U.N.C.L.E. car behind the building and entered the back door, Illya had made a cautious tour of the premises and was confident that only one watchman had been on duty.

"If we had any doubts about Thrush's involvement before, this should dispel them," Illya held the Thrush communicator in the beam of his flashlight.

Napoleon glanced at it briefly. "Weapons?" he inquired.

"A .455 Webley revolver, of all things," Illya replied. "I didn't know Thrush went in for buying war surplus."

"Maybe somebody got a bargain. It's comforting to think of them having to justify expenditures, too. But right now we had best get busy looking for the drug."

Illya swung his light over the cluttered back room in which they stood. "Any tampering would be done here. There's a passageway and some offices in front. The upstairs seems to have been used entirely for storage."

The two agents separated and worked their way through the clutter. Several minutes later they met at a long bench near the center of the room. "This would seem to be it," Napoleon said. "The jugs of syrup over by the stairway have the seals intact, probably the way they were received from the manufacturer. And here we have several that have obviously been opened."

Illya swung his light along the bench, bare except for the half dozen jugs of syrup. "So they're opened here and then resealed, with the magic ingredient added." He squatted down and looked under the bench. What appeared to be a rusty toolbox rested on the floor. "Here's something," he said, pulling it out from under the bench and setting it on top.

Napoleon stared at it for a moment, then laid his flashlight down and tried to lift the toolbox lid. When it became apparent it wasn't going to budge, Illya produced his picklock again and went to work. The tool box was much more difficult to open than the back door had been, but something finally clicked and the lid came up easily. The inside was in perfect condition, in contrast to the rusted outer surface. Six small sealed cannisters sat in a wooden rack.

Illya took one out and carefully unscrewed the cap, then shook a small portion of the contents onto the bench.

"Lavender?" Napoleon peered closely at the colorful powder. "I never suspected that esthetics entered into drug manufacturing."

Illya wet a forefinger and dabbed it into the powder,

then brought the finger to his nose to sniff. "No odor," he reported as he eyed his lavender fingertip. "Considering its already proven effect on me, I don't think I'll test it for flavor. Besides, I wouldn't know what the drug tasted like anyway."

"I think we can assume this is the drug," Napoleon said. "What we had better do, though, is get some of it back to the lab for analysis." He pulled a small test tube from a jacket pocket, filled it from the cannister and carefully stoppered it.

Illya, who had been looking about speculatively as Napoleon filled the test tube, looked back at the six cannisters. "Why not take all of it?" he asked.

Napoleon shook his head. "No need for more than a sample to analyze. We'd better destroy the remainder, though. Any suggestions as to how? Pouring it down the sink doesn't seem too practical. You never know where a town's old, used water is going to show up next."

"Burning would be easiest, if it will burn. I saw something that looked like a trash burner out in the yard."

Napoleon looked around the littered room again. "Thrush has become rather messy lately. You think we can do it without setting the whole place on fire? Remember what Mr. Waverly says about wanton destruction of property, even when we *are* reasonably sure it belongs to Thrush."

"I know. He's been rather sensitive on the subject since you blew a hole in that poor woman's bedroom floor to get at Dr. Morthley. But the burner is away from the building, and I don't see any other quick way."

Napoleon gathered the six cannisters and the small pile of powder from the workbench and headed for the back yard. Illya grabbed one of the jugs of opened syrup and followed. In the back yard, Illya found an open space that looked like it would soak up the syrup while Napoleon started a fire in the trash burner. A minute later, he dumped the contents of one of the cannisters into the flame and was rewarded with a blinding green flash that approximated seasick daylight.

"If it has that many calories, it must be fattening, too," Napoleon remarked as he hurriedly dumped in the rest of the powder and waited for the glare to die down. By the time Illya had dumped all the jugs of syrup, Napoleon's vision had cleared and he could make out the car several yards away.

They were just starting toward the car when the yard was suddenly swept by headlights turning into the drive. "Word gets around fast," Illya remarked as they broke into a sprint for the car.

The oncoming vehicle skidded to a stop on the gravel and began disgorging armed men who were firing as they emerged. Illya and Napoleon were just able to make it to the cover of their car as the bullets began striking around them and whining off the car. From behind the car, Napoleon returned the fire with his U.N.-C.L.E. Special while Illya got out the Mercox and fitted it with one of the high explosive projectiles. He fired quickly; a second later there was an answering explosion and the car's lights went out. Illya hurriedly reloaded the Mercox with a tear gas projectile.

"Get ready to move when I fire this one," he said, pulling the trigger a split second later. There was a slight popping sound, and Thrush fire rapidly slackened, to be replaced by violent coughing and choking sounds.

"Now!" Illya shouted, wrenching open the door and leaping inside. Napoleon jumped for the door on the passenger's side and made it just as a final shot from a determined Thrush sent a bullet whining off the hood.

Illya got the car moving before switching on the headlights to reveal a number of red-eyed Thrushes diving for cover behind their car. The car itself was little better off, its hood crumpled and a large puddle of something under the radiator. Napoleon glanced back as they roared past. "Haven't I seen a couple of those faces before?"

"At the Fort Wayne airport, yelling 'U.N.C.L.E., go home!'" Illya confirmed as he swung the car onto the long driveway that led to the highway. He reached the end of the driveway and was pausing to let a fast moving car by when he realized that it was not going by but headed directly at them. The glint of an automatic was visible outside the right front window and a bullet thudded against the rear of the car.

"Reinforcements," Illya muttered as he floored the accelerator. In a matter of seconds, the U.N.C.L.E. car began to pull away. Several ineffective shots came from the pursuing car.

"Whither away?" Napoleon inquired as Illya negotiated a curve with an expert, if stomach twisting, controlled skid.

"Anyplace I can find a straight road," Illya replied, braking suddenly and swinging onto a blacktop road that intersected the highway. At the same moment, he gave one of the buttons on the dashboard a quick jab. A cloud of smoke billowed out behind them, obscuring the intersection. "They should have fun making that turn," he remarked.

Napoleon looked at him admiringly. "You're developing a very creditable mean streak," he said.

Illya concentrated on negotiating another curve. As he slid into it, he could see the Thrush car emerging from the cloud. "Now that we're on a side road, how about the laser system?" he asked.

Napoleon peered backward for a moment, then shook his head. "I'm not well enough checked out on that thing to try hitting something on these curves. And on a straight road, we won't need it."

Illya nodded. All he really needed was a few miles of straight road; he felt sure he could run away from anything on the road.

Signs warned of an intersecting highway. Illya braked

again and swung onto it. The pursuit took the corner on two wheels and almost ended up in the ditch, but the driver fought the car back under control and continued. There were more curves and then Illya grinned as the car topped a low hill and the headlights revealed a long expanse of straightaway, with no other cars in sight. He floored the accelerator again and simultaneously cut in the car's high speed supercharged exhaust system. On either side, berm and fencerows became a gray blur. Behind, the Thrush car dropped steadily further back but continued to pursue.

"If this just holds out a little longer," Illya murmured hopefully. "We'll have—"

The car swooped over the crest of a hill and he saw that the road was totally blocked just ahead.

Chapter 11

"Who Ever Heard Of A Flying Saucer With A Parachute"

A SIGN READING "Beaver Dam, Pop. 862" went by in a blur as Illya and Napoleon bore down on a street fair that stretched along the highway for blocks. Reacting automatically, Illya simultaneously shut off the afterburner, punched the button to fire the braking parachute, and applied the conventional brakes. The savage jolt as the chute took hold almost threw the car off the road, but Illya managed to hold it under control as their speed dropped below 100.

At 50, he discarded the parachute and a second later skidded around a corner on screaming tires, still a half block from the near edge of the street fair. A block off the highway, he came to another street running parallel to the highway. Now at normal speed, Illya turned onto it and found himself confronted by an extension of the fair. A large, darkened tent loomed invitingly at the next intersection, and without hesitating, Illya drove inside. The two agents paused only long enough to let out their breath, which they realized they had been holding since they came over the last hill, then got out and locked the car.

"I take it we stay here while the pursuit goes merrily by," Napoleon said as they walked out of the tent and carefully closed the flaps behind them.

A sudden crash, followed by an outburst of shouting came from the general direction of the highway. "The pursuit doesn't seem to be very merry at the moment," Napoleon commented.

"Let's hope that was the only car," Illya said as he started to trot forward a little faster. "I saw another pair of headlights back there once, I think. At the speed we were going, it had to be either Thrush or some local hot rodder who wanted to race."

By now they were merging with the crowd that swarmed over the brightly lighted highway. The Thrush car, obviously going at a good speed and lacking a parachute brake, hadn't been able to stop in time. At the last minute, the driver had managed to avoid the ferris wheel but had steered into what proved to be a livestock tent. While the lone passenger indulged in a nose-to-nose confrontation with an annoyed cow, the driver was arguing with a local law officer, apparently the sheriff.

"But dammit, you're blocking a state highway!" the driver was shouting.

The sheriff looked as unimpressed as the livestock. "Son, we've been blocking this highway for our Muck Crop Festival for twenty years. We've got a court order saying we can block this highway. Now then, I know how much space you had to stop in and you didn't make it. You can have your choice—speeding or defective brakes. Which will it be?"

Meanwhile, another hubbub was breaking out on the fringes of the crowd. Someone had spotted the parachute lying at the side of the street almost a block away. "I *told* you I saw a parachute!" someone was saying indignantly.

"And there was a little round ship that came down with it!" another chimed in. "It made a terrible screaming noise as it came down and I saw port holes and a strange yellow man in it."

"Yeh, me too," said a third. "It just hovered there for a minute and shot out of sight over the trees."

"Don't be silly," someone else said. "Who ever heard of a flying saucer with a parachute?"

"What's wrong with a parachute?" the first man asked, still sounding huffy. "That's how *our* space capsules come down. Why shouldn't theirs?"

"What would a flying saucer want to observe a Muck Crop Festival for?" a bewildered individual asked. "What does it all mean?"

At this point, another car came tearing over the hill and came to a lurching, tire-squealing stop halfway between the parachute and the ferris wheel. The driver got out quickly and headed for the first car. The sheriff waved to him as he walked past where he was slowly and deliberately writing out a ticket for the driver of the first car.

"Good brakes there, son," the sheriff said cheerfully. The driver of the second car smiled weakly and went up to the first car, nudging the cow out of his way. After exchanging a few words with the passenger, he left and headed directly for the spot where the U.N.-C.L.E. agents were standing.

Illya and Napoleon hastily faded into an alley and ducked around the corner of a garage as the Thrush also entered the alley and pulled out a communicator. He spoke quietly into it, instructing all units to converge on Beaver Dam. "Cover all roads between here and Midford," he concluded. "They'll have to take one of them."

"Maybe waiting it out wasn't such a good idea," Illya suggested as the Thrush disappeared back into the crowd.

"We're all right as long as they don't decide to look in the wrong tent," Napoleon replied. "Incidentally, which way is Midford from here?"

Illya shrugged. "I wasn't paying attention to direction, just distance. We'll have to look it up on a map, I suppose." He looked around as they reentered the milling crowd. "But there's no rush. Let's wait till Thrush has run itself out. As long as we're here, let's not pass up an opportunity to find out what a Muck Crop Festival is. It's part of our national heritage."

Napoleon declined to comment on a national heritage that would include something called a Muck Crop Festival. After a half hour, the only thing that had attracted his attention favorably was a grandstand full of girls in bathing suits. A leather-lunged announcer was shouting to all and sundry that the final judging for the Muck Queen was about to begin.

"If this weren't a wholesome midwestern town, I'd be suspicious," Napoleon commented. "Just what *is* muck, anyway, that it gets to have a festival and a queen all to itself?"

"A kind of soil," Illya said. "Very rich, but highly unpleasant to work with. Like glue when it's wet, but it grows great crops. It's similar to having a Peat Bog Festival and electing a Miss Peat Bog, I suppose."

Napoleon still looked dubious. "Probably all part of a Thrush scheme," he remarked darkly. "Speaking of which, don't you think pursuit has passed us by? If it's going to, that is?"

"We should give them a little longer, but it won't hurt to check all the streets leading out of town while we're waiting."

They spent an hour exploring the streets of Beaver Dam on foot before returning to their car, where Illya intently studied a local map for a minute. "They can't cover everything unless they have a larger force than we've seen so far," he decided. "Especially with two of their cars out of action. If we leave town on the side away from Midford and make a long detour, we may be safe enough."

Illya eased the car out of the tent and cruised quietly down the side street. They had gone only a few blocks when red lights began flashing at a railroad crossing ahead of them. Illya stopped next to an alley and they waited as a seemingly endless freight train rumbled by at a snail's pace. The train was still moving past when Napoleon nudged Illya and pointed across the street.

"A man walking along there saw us and ducked behind that tree. I suspect that pursuit may not have entirely passed us by after all."

Illya promptly swung the car into the alley. A shot sounded behind them but there was no other evidence of pursuit. He turned into the next street and drove rapidly. Several blocks down, a man carrying what could have been either a length of water pipe or a bazooka looked up intently. Illya took no chances and made a sharp U-turn. As he straightened out again, Napoleon pointed ahead.

"That's the number two car that was after us earlier," he announced.

Illya made another turn into an intersecting street and the car picked up speed. Behind them the sounds of the chase mounted. Ahead, moonlight glinted on water. "Always have an extra bolt hole," he said and drove straight ahead.

They came to the end of the street, bounced over a low curb, crashed through a wooden fence, crossed a small park and stretch of beach and plunged into the waters of Beaver Lake. As they hit the water, Illya

110

dropped their twin propellors into place and the car chugged out into the water at a moderate speed. Behind them, there was first a stunned silence, then much shouting and the sound of squealing tires as the cars turned around. As a precaution, Napoleon raised the bullet proof shield to protect their rear from shorebound sharpshooters.

"If they don't have a navy," said Illya confidently, "we should be all right. The lake is rather narrow here, but it's a drive of several miles around by road. We can be well on our way before they get around."

The remainder of the drive was routine. Lem Thompson, however, did not consider anything that roused him from a sound sleep at midnight to be either routine or bearable. He looked grumpily at Illya but agreed to hide him out. Agreeing was easier than arguing at this time of night.

"One more thing," Napoleon added. "We have to get this sample to the Fort Wayne airport, and I'm sure they'll be watching for this car. Could you see that Illya gets there?"

"And what if Illya's watched, too? Gimme the samples, and I'll take 'em myself. Gonna rain tomorrow anyway, so I won't be able to get any *real* work done." Lem clumped off, muttering that in *his* day people did their own work without always having to be helped out.

Napoleon smiled at Illya. "You just have to know how to handle people," he said as he got back into the car and headed for Whateley's.

Ten minutes later, Napoleon swung the U.N.C.L.E. car into the Whateley driveway and parked at the side of the house. As he started around to the front, a bright, flickering light from one of the basement windows caught his eye. Thoughts of devil worship and eldritch rites briefly crossed his mind, but he quickly decided that the light was much too bright for that kind of thing. By the time he reached the front door, he realized it must be Flavia pursuing her hobby. His thoughts pleasantly balanced between idle conversation with a pretty girl and pumping a possible source of information, Napoleon entered the house and went down the stairs to Flavia's studio.

Attired in jeans, sweatshirt, a heavy canvas apron, and oversized goggles, she was using an acetylene torch to attach a gaudy red metal bird to an assembly already supporting a dozen identical creatures. When she had the bird firmly attached, she looked around and, seeing Napoleon, smiled and shut off the torch.

"Don't let me disturb you," he said.

"Oh, this is nothing important," she said. "Just an eyebrow raiser for a local art show." When Napoleon looked puzzled, she went on. "Not the work itself, but the title. In a moment of weakness, I decided to call it Collage of Cardinals."

Napoleon grimaced dutifully. "If you enjoy raising eyebrows, there must be ways that are less work." He looked around the basement studio. "Just living in this house would be enough for most. All it needs are a few cobwebs at strategic locations to turn it into a horror movie set."

Flavia laughed. "It's already been a horror movie set, if you count amateur productions. The university drama club wrote and directed a movie last year and shot the scenes here; and believe me, it was a horror. This was right after Father put up the TV station and was trying to be a pillar of the community. I'm afraid he's just not cut out for the part, though."

"You can take the boy out of demonology, but you can never take demonology out of the boy," Napoleon volunteered. "Is he really serious about all this devil worship and calling up old gods?"

She smiled faintly. "He's just joking, of course," she said, a trifle emphatically. "Although I admit his sense of humor is a little odd; sometimes his jokes even frighten me a little. Rita is the only one who really enjoys them; sometimes I think she wouldn't be frightened if he was serious. Of course, since the TV station, the rest of the town tries to be polite and not offend him."

"I don't blame them," Napoleon said. "If I really believed that one of my acquaintances could call up demons, I'd try not to offend him, either. That's about the same impression I got from the newspapers. Most of the articles lent themselves very well to reading between the lines." At her questioning look, he recounted his research into local history.

"I'd forgotten that book," Flavia said, "although Father has two or three copies in the library. He was quite proud of it."

"Did Jabez, Senior, really duplicate the New England mansion?" he asked. "Or is that just another wild story?"

"It's reasonably close, I understand," Flavia replied. "Secret passages and all. Of course, I never saw the original. The New England branch of our family has gone modern and the old house was sold years ago."

"Secret passages?" Napoleon said, pricking his ears.

"Oh yes, the place is honeycombed with them. Weren't they mentioned in that book you read? I'm sure they were in some book. They've never been terribly secret in the sense that nobody knows they exist; they're just hard to locate, even if you know about them. The traditional method of making passages really secret is to kill off all the workmen who install them, and Grandfather never did anything like that, despite what you may read. In fact, one of the family stories is that he included them because he liked to get away from Grandmother now and then. Here, I'll show you."

She walked around the workbench and the blacksmith's forge next to it. Going up to what looked like a solid wall, she began poking at various points. After a minute's experimentation, she stepped back and a three foot section of the wall swung out into the room.

"Amazing," Napoleon said as he peered into the blackened opening. "Where does it go?"

Flavia chuckled. "Where doesn't it go? You can reach almost any room in the house through these. A few were lost when father installed central heating and used them for hot air ducts, but there are still entrances in most of the bedrooms, the living room, and the study."

"How about the kitchen?" Napoleon inquired.

"None there. Grandfather said he had a hard enough time keeping cooks, without providing secret exits for them. But the rest of the house is pretty well covered."

She stepped back from the opening and it slid smoothly closed. As they returned to the center of the room, she asked, unexpectedly. "I don't suppose you have any photos of Illya? I really would like to get him into metal. And besides," she smiled, "I have a feeling it would be terribly commercial."

Napoleon shook his head. "I'm afraid secret agents don't carry photos of one another in their wallets; risky, you know. But I'm sure Illya would send you one if you really want it."

"He has a face that would sell," Flavia said. "I'm sure my agent could get a few hundred for it, at least."

"It's a good hobby that makes money," Napoleon observed. "I didn't realize there was that much of a market for metal sculpture."

"That's why I need an agent; he has contacts with art dealers all over the country. Actually, of course, I don't make a lot of money; there are shipping charges to pay, for one thing." She swung her arm around to encompass a half dozen projects, none of which could have weighed less than a hundred pounds and most of which weighed more. "If I could make a living at it, I'd be in New York. I'll make it, one of these days."

Napoleon stifled a yawn and looked at his watch. "You seem to have the true artistic temperament as regards night-time work," he observed. "I'm going to have a busy day tomorrow with Illya gone. I think I'll turn in."

Flavia nodded understandingly. "I think I'll get started on a bust of Illya from memory, just in case I don't get a photo." She paused thoughtfully. "In fact, it may be better this way. You know how reality never lives up to memories."

Napoleon looked somewhat blank, and departed. Back in his room, he began examining the walls, tilting pictures, and moving the furniture. It took him only a short time to discover that either the bed was more massive than it looked or it was fastened to the floor. After that, it took somewhat longer to locate the two patterns in the scrollwork of the bedpost that concealed tiny switches. A minute later he was standing in an opening that had appeared in one wall when both switches were pressed simultaneously.

The passage was relatively wide and evidently cleaned often enough to keep dust and cobwebs from piling up. It led to a stairway that descended all the way to the basement. At the ground floor level, a passageway similar to the one on the second floor opened off the stairway. There were two connecting passages at the basement level.

Napoleon laboriously followed each passage in turn. At the end of an hour he had discovered absolutely nothing except for some hot air ducts and several miles of electrical wiring and water pipes. Having secret passages running though most of the house, he decided, could be very useful in such everyday matters as electricity and plumbing. And that, apparently, was all this entire rabbit warren of passages was used for. It seemed unimaginative for someone of Whateley's inclinations.

Napoleon was standing quietly in one of the passages, trying to think of a positive course of action, when a sudden noise just behind him jarred him from his reverie. Automatically he turned his flashlight toward the sound and whipped out his U.N.C.L.E. Special pistol. Slightly chagrined to find himself facing a blank wall, he put away the pistol and listened more closely. Obviously, someone was in the room beyond.

Cautiously, Napoleon examined the wall in front of him. The passageways had been designed to allow observation of the rooms. With characteristic conservatism, Whateley had used the old peephole in the picture trick in most rooms—although, Napoleon had to admit, it might have not been such an old trick when the house was built. There were none into this room, however, though there was the usual hidden door.

For several minutes there were no further sounds from the other side of the wall, but Napoleon waited. The only logical room from which to omit peepholes would be the one used exclusively by the master of the house. Coupled with Napoleon's vague idea of his position in the house, this made it seem likely that he was standing just outside Jabez Whateley's study; which in turn meant that the individual who had made the noise a few minutes earlier was probably Jabez Whateley himself.

There was a squeaking noise, like that of an unoiled swivel chair, then silence again. Napoleon had almost decided to give up his vigil and get some sleep when there was a faint buzzing sound. It was a sound he had heard often enough before: the signal tone of a Thrush communicator.

Section IV : "Likewise, Give The Victor A Cheer"

Chapter 12

"I Don't Care If They Flapped Their Wings And Flew"

NAPOLEON PRESSED HIS EAR tightly against the concealed door and tried to breathe quietly.

"Whateley here," a voice from the other end of the wall said. "Report."

The reply over the communicator was too low for Napoleon to hear, but it was evidently unsatisfactory. Whateley's voice came again, sharply.

"You aren't being paid to make excuses. You're being paid, and paid well, I might add, to produce results." Listening to the sepulchral overtones, Napoleon found himself beginning to sympathize with the Thrush underling. There was more muttering from the communicator, but Whateley cut it short.

"I don't care if they flapped their wings and flew away! You were told they were dangerous and inventive, and you were instructed to be prepared for anything. So far, all you've accomplished is to lose two cars and get one driver in jail for attempting to bribe an officer."

The muttering began to take on an indignant tone. Whateley broke in again. "It's nice to know you can do one thing right, at least. Transfer some of those men to—what?" There was some apologetic muttering, and Whateley let out a strangled noise. "On a simple job like that! Do you think I get replacements by magic? Get back to base and stay there; we don't have enough cars left to allow you to be roaming the highways in them. I'll have further orders later."

There was a click as the communicator cover was flipped shut, followed by another squeak of the chair and the sound of footsteps pacing about the room. Napoleon hastily retreated down the passage and up two steps. Whateley was apparently planning his next move; it would be inconvenient if the next move turned out to be opening the secret door of his study and coming face to face with Napoleon Solo. Before there were any such encounters, Napoleon wanted to find the source of the lavender drug. Keeping one ear open for the sound of Whateley's door, Napoleon took out his communicator and softly called Illya.

Illya's response was instant and acid. "Don't you ever go to bed?"

"I'm doing my share of the skulking." Napoleon repeated his discoveries, including the operation of the hidden doors in his room and Flavia's studio. "I'm going to do some further exploring. I'll keep in touch; if you haven't heard from me again by morning, you're on your own. But these passages must lead somewhere." Illya agreed to pass the information along to Waverly.

After concluding the conversation, Napoleon sat down on the steps to think. He was almost certain that these passageways were somehow connected with a Thrush stronghold. It would seem a remarkable waste of available facilities by Whateley if they were not. But where was the connection? He had been over every passage and had found nothing, not even a dirt smudge on a wall that might mark a concealed lever. Of course, any extension of the passageways into a Thrush base would be well hidden, since Flavia said that the existence of the passages he was in was not much of a secret. There was a chance that shadowing Whateley would lead him to something. Unfortunately, shadowing a man in his own house—particularly a house like this—was an extremely risky procedure.

Napoleon stared glumly at the wall in front of him. What else could he do? There had to be an extension of the passages somewhere, and apparently Jabez Whateley was the only one who knew where. In that case, there might be a clue to the secret in Whateley's study. Certainly it couldn't be anywhere else. In fact why couldn't the controls be in Whateley's study? The door controls had been modernized at some time, and all the secret doors he had found were operated by small electric motors controlled by hidden switches. A remote control in the study would make sense; any prowlers like himself could search the passageways to their heart's content without learning anything useful—as he had just done.

He got up from the step and moved quietly down the passage until he was once again outside Whateley's study. There was not a sound from the other side of the wall. He waited cautiously for several minutes until he was satisfied that Whateley had left the study, then operated the manual lever that controlled the secret door from the passageway side. He entered, ready with an explanation if Whateley should, against expectations, be inside. After all, Flavia had showed him an entrance to the passages; now that he was sure that this portion of them was innocuous, he doubted that Whateley would do anything drastic.

The precaution was needless; the study was empty. Napoleon discovered that he had entered the room from behind a section of bookcase which swung out. Another example of traditionalism, he noted. He carefully closed the door and swept the beam of his flashlight around the room. It contained a desk, chairs, the bookcases, what appeared to be the master control panel for Whateley's intercom system, and more of the morbid artwork. A well-worn but comfortable-looking couch stood in one corner.

Napoleon made for the desk, but before he could examine it he heard the sound of muffled footsteps. He started for the door, decided that the footsteps were probably coming from the hallway, and turned back to the room. As the footsteps grew louder, he climbed over the couch and dropped into the narrow space behind it. By now the footsteps were close, but he still couldn't be sure whether they came from the hallway or the secret passage.

There was a click and light spilled across the floor and fell on the couch. Napoleon realized with mounting excitement that it came from neither the hall nor the secret door that he had recently used, but from a different side of the room entirely. The footsteps entered the study. Peering around the end of the couch, Napoleon heard another click, and witnessed a section of wall swing shut. Closed, it appeared to be simply a section containing a large, built-in television screen.

Whoever had come through the wall didn't bother to turn on lights in the study. He walked briskly to the desk, opened one of the drawers, and deposited an object inside. Then he left; Napoleon heard his retreating footsteps in the hall outside. They faded to silence.

Napoleon started breathing again and slowly pulled himself out from behind the couch. Deciding he might have very little time, he pulled out his flashlight and approached the desk. A quick search through the drawers revealed what he was after; a seemingly ordinary remote control unit for a TV set. He slid the desk drawers closed and walked over to the TV screen. Considering the haste with which Whateley had deposited the unit in the desk, Napoleon hoped he had not reset the controls.

He was right; the section of wall containing the TV screen swung out smoothly when he pressed the "on" button, and he just had time to drop the unit back in the desk drawer when he heard footsteps in the hall outside. A key rattled in the hallway door as Napoleon ran softly across the room and ducked through the opening. Once through, he reached back and tried to pull it shut. At first it jammed, and he began wondering if he should run and hope that Whateley would think he absent-mindedly left the door open. But, as the hall door began to swing open, Napoleon's tugs achieved results and the section of wall closed silently. He rather doubted that it latched, for he didn't hear the distinctive click that had come when Whateley closed it, but it was just as well. With Whateley coming through the door, the click of the latch would have brought him into the passageway on the run.

Napoleon drew his U.N.C.L.E. Special and held it ready while he listened through the wall for sounds of Whateley's approach. The only sound, however, was that of the desk chair squeaking. After a minute of tense silence, Napoleon looked around. Unlike the other passages, this one was reasonably well lighted. A bare bulb hung from the ceiling, illuminating a stairway. Moving silently, Napoleon descended the stairs. At the basement level, the passage diverged, one branch going straight ahead, the other to his right. He started down the righthand passage, keeping a careful watch for possible Thrushes. The passage grew dimmer as he left the illuminated junction, but it moved straight ahead until it abruptly ended in a blank wall. Napoleon put away his gun and was reaching for his flashlight when there was a clattering sound from the wall on his right.

He froze. The clattering and crashing continued. It

sounded, he decided, like someone moving a pile of old lumber. He glanced at his watch. The Whateleys appeared to be a remarkably nocturnal clan. The clatter stopped, and he could hear someone moving around in the basement. He reached into his pocket and pulled out his flashlight; there was the clatter of something at his feet. Looking down, he saw the offending object; his communicator. It had apparently been snagged by the flashlight when he had pulled the latter out of his pocket.

He stood silently and there was an equal silence from the opposite side of the wall. Napoleon now saw a small door on the basement side of the passage, but there was no time to investigate it. Whoever was in the basement approached the wall. There was a faint scraping sound as though inquisitive hands were being moved over it. He picked up his communicator and moved away as quietly as he could.

As he reached the junction, he noticed that these passages were walled with different, newer material, unlike the passages in the house. There wasn't the musty odor of age that prevailed in the other passages, either. Presumably these had been added by the younger Jabez, probably with the help of Thrush. He wondered if Flavia knew about them or if she was as innocent as she appeared to be.

After a distance of about forty feet, the main passage changed into a hallway, with doors on each side. In the distance he could see an intersecting corridor. The second door off the hall was not only open, there was a light in the room. Cautiously, Napoleon approached the open door and listened. He could make out a hissing sound, but that was all. After a minute he risked a quick glance into the room.

A well-stocked chemical laboratory greeted his gaze. Cabinets filled with hundreds of bottled chemicals lined one wall, and racks of test tubes, flasks, ring stands, bunsen burners and other lab equipment were in cabinets and on benches along the other two walls. On one of the benches, a half-full flask sat bubbling on a ring stand over the pointed blue flame of a bunsen burner.

Napoleon quickly checked the hallway. No one was in sight. He stepped inside the lab and pulled out his communicator. In a whisper, he reported his find to Illya.

"Good work," Illya said. "I always told you that skillful skulking pays off. Do you think he's brewing another batch of the drug?"

"Probably, but I can't really tell. It's not lavender, but on the other hand, it isn't a powder, either. From what I overheard earlier, our destruction of the supply of drugs at the vending company has been reported. So the logical thing for him to do would be to brew up another batch as quickly as possible. If what happened to Armden when he was taken off the drug is typical, it would seem that dosage must be continuous."

Illya agreed. "What are your plans?"

"I'll try to ambush Whateley when he returns; he left all the lights on and the burner going, so presumably he's coming back. I don't have any equipment to get information out of him, so about all I can do is hang onto him—unless he decides to talk voluntarily. You relay this to Mr. Waverly and get over here with some truth serum. Once we have the formula and manufacturing process from Whateley, the lab boys can come up with an antidote."

"I'll notify Mr. Waverly right away," Illya said, "but it may be a little while before I can get to you. Lem took the only serviceable vehicle on the farm to Fort Wayne with the drug samples, and you have the U.N.-C.L.E. car there."

"All right," Napoleon said. "Get here as soon as you can. I'll try to hold the fort until you arrive."

Napoleon had just closed the communicator and returned it to his pocket when the lights went out. He was left in darkness illuminated only by the blue flame of the bunsen burner. He started to pull out his flashlight but thought better of it. The lights had been put out deliberately; his flashlight would make a perfect target. Instead, he pulled out his gun and began cautiously feeling his way toward the doorway to the hall. He was almost there when Jabez Whateley's sepulchral voice came from somewhere in the blackness.

"I have infra-red goggles and can see you perfectly, Mr. Solo. Kindly refrain from any motion whatsoever."

Chapter 13

"How Does 'Whateley For President' Strike You?"

NAPOLEON FROZE, the U.N.C.L.E. Special still in his hand. Whateley chuckled, the sound echoing hollowly in the underground room so that Napoleon was unable to tell where the Thrush leader was standing. The eerie voice came again.

"You're doing fine, Mr. Solo. Stand perfectly still while I pull your fangs."

An invisible hand removed his pistol and a second later delved into his pocket and removed his communicator and the other pen-sized devices he carried there, plus his flashlight.

"Now then, Mr. Solo, I'm sure you still have a few other lethal items about your person, so I warn you; don't even twitch unless I tell you to. It is expedient to keep you alive for the present, but not at all necessary. Now, clasp your hands behind your head. That's right, clasped tightly."

There was a click and the lights came back on.

Whateley was standing a few feet from Napoleon, holding a rectangular device similar to the unit that opened the secret panel in his study in one hand and a Mossin-Nagant revolver in the other. He put down the remote-control light switch long enough to strip off the infra-red goggles and lay them on a bench, then motioned with the revolver.

"Walk slowly ahead of me."

Following his captor's directions, Napoleon walked down the corridor past the other doors. At the intersecting corridor, he was directed to turn left; he shortly found himself in a gloomy passage with unfinished stone walls and a damp concrete floor. At a barred door, he halted and faced the wall while Whateley opened the door; then he was marched through and down a short flight of steps to a dungeon-like area, with sturdy cells flanking the walls and an open area in the center containing various instruments. Napoleon recognized a rack, a charcoal brazier with tongs, and an iron maiden. He failed to recognize other implements which looked equally unpleasant.

"As you see," Whateley remarked, "even in my information-gathering techniques, I am something of a traditionalist. However, you may consider yourself fortunate, Mr. Solo, for I do not require any information from you. Now then, over into that open cell on your left."

Napoleon complied, and extended his hands back through the bars as he was instructed. Whateley handcuffed his wrists together and stepped back to admire his handiwork.

"That should render you reasonably harmless, but just to make sure . . ." Whateley produced a roll of adhesive tape from somewhere and taped Napoleon's wrists together. "That should take care of any little tricks you might have left. I feel much more comfortable now."

Napoleon nodded at the revolver, which Whateley was transferring from his belt to a coat pocket. "Does the Russian armament have any significance, or is Thrush merely flaunting its international status?"

Whateley shook his head. "No, the head of a certain European satrapy was offered a bargain in military arms." He looked at the weapon distastefully. "Naturally, the stuff eventually got dumped on us. Whenever Thrush Central finds itself with material it doesn't know what to do with, we get it. Just because this is largely a rural satrapy, they think they can get away with anything. We were getting nothing but Volkswagens until I put my foot down. Of course, it's a nice little car, but it has certain drawbacks for our work. It's really amazing what they try to palm off on us; once they even tried to give us a second-hand dirigible. Can you imagine it?"

Napoleon nodded solemnly. "I know how it is. You wouldn't believe the sort of thing we at U.N.C.L.E. have to go through to get a simple expense account approved."

"Oh, yes I would," replied Whateley. "I have the same problems. I know the official position is that Thrush is a free-wheeling organization, throwing millions around in a quest for world domination, but you'd never know it by working in the Central Indiana Satrapy. I've sent Thrush Central four requisitions for cyanide in the past month, and do you think I've seen any of it? Not a gram!"

"You might try conjuring it up," Napoleon offered.

Whateley produced his sinister smile. "I suspect that you aren't entirely convinced by the insistence of Rita and Flavia that my demonology is merely a pose. It isn't, of course. What better place to hide a serious interest in demons and gods than under an opera cape and theatrical gestures? Nobody believes in that sort of thing any more, and so anything I may be seen doing is simply explained as another example of my melodramatic nature. In fact, my father and uncle were the last full time practitioners. There are easier ways of obtaining power than by invoking malign and capricious entities which would be as much inclined to kill me as to obey my orders. It's much simpler to invoke Thrush, red tape and all." He paused reflectively. "My cousins tried a different method. I understand they made an alliance with some Irishman and went into politics."

Whateley paused again.

"I thought you said the old gods were so powerful that mankind could not resist them," Napoleon said. "Thrush doesn't have that kind of power."

"It will, Mr. Solo; it will. However, there is the problem of communicating with the old gods and of striking a bargain with them. Their history does not show them to be particularly trustworthy and there are very few ways to force a god to obey one's will. In any event, one does not invoke them lightly. For general use, the standard, or garden variety of demon, is sufficient. Even they, however, are not particularly reliable."

"Does Flavia know about all this? She's a good actress if she does; she sounded as if she really believed that your demonology was a pose."

"Oh, she does, just as Miss Berman does. I cultivate that opinion, of course. However, Flavia is becoming something of a problem. When she was younger, we operated differently and she didn't question my being away from home a lot. We put in this underground base while she was away at school. I wasn't expecting her to return and set up shop in the basement; I expected her to find some nice young man and settle down somewhere. As it is, I hope her work starts selling well; I've offered to pay her expenses if she will live in New York, but she insists on being able to pay her own way. I'm considering priming the pump, so to speak; a few good purchases through a third party should do the job. If it doesn't, I'll have to, ah, consider other solutions."

Whateley took out his pocket watch. "I can't stay much longer; I must attend to other business, such as preparing a nice warm cell for your friend Mr. Kuryakin."

Napoleon looked surprised. "But Illya is in New York by now."

"Now, now, Mr. Solo, we know better than that, don't we? For one thing, Lem Thompson's farm has been under surveillance since yesterday. For another, I overheard your recent conversation with the dear boy. My intercom system," he gestured at an overhead speaker with a bony finger, "is also designed to pick up sounds from any room and broadcast them on a special frequency to my communicator. I can tune in to any room that I wish." He held up his Thrush communicator proudly.

"Handy gadget," Napoleon said. The longer he could keep Whateley talking, the more chance there was of discovering something that he could use to turn the tables on the Thrush. "But it seems a bit odd to have it set up here as well as the house, here in secret passages that no one but Thrush uses."

Whateley chuckled again. "Although I find Thrush an admirable organization, dealing with individuals entirely devoid of principle does require some discretion. For example, I am the discoverer of the drug that you and Mr. Kuryakin are so interested in. I am also the only man in the world who knows how to make it. Anyone with a good laboratory could analyze its composition, of course, but they might be a little surprised if they tried to duplicate it." He smiled. "Like so many modern drugs, the secret is in the manufacturing process and I doubt that anyone could duplicate mine. I doubt that many people would even believe mine. But, as I started to say, this gives me a much securer niche in the organization than most Thrush satrapy heads possess."

"An astute maneuver," Napoleon said admiringly. "I assume you also invented the rather complicated system of administering the drug and the subliminal conditioning?"

Whateley leaned back against the iron maiden and smiled, looking as if he would be happy to lecture Napoleon for the rest of the night.

"Actually," he said, "the administration and conditioning were determined by the action of the drug. As you have no doubt guessed, its entire effect is to make people susceptible to suggestion, but both the dosage and the conditioning must be gradual for the best results. Drugging the drinks in Falco's vending machines was an ideal method of administration: half a dozen times a day, five days a week. In the early stages there is a tendency for the subject to regress over weekends; in the long run this is unimportant, but it enabled you to talk Armden into going with you. If you had arrived in the middle of the week, you would never have convinced him. As I was saying, it is the subconscious of the subject that we must work on. Direct orders are not feasible, while subliminal conditioning works wonders."

Napoleon looked puzzled. "But Illya and Dr. Armden obeyed direct orders when they were drugged the other day."

"Ah, but they had been given a massive dose. Such a dose does enable the subject to respond to direct orders; unfortunately he doesn't respond to anything else. His will power is temporarily destroyed. We want to obtain scientists with their initiative and creativity intact. Also, conflicting orders given to anyone with a massive dose of the drug produce hysteria and collapse, as you observed in Dr. Armden's reactions last Monday. I would have preferred not to give him that dose, but you forced our hand."

"But wouldn't normal brainwashing techniques accomplish the same thing?" Napoleon asked. "You have all sorts to choose from, from the Chinese to Madison Avenue."

"I'm afraid not. Efficient brainwashing requires that the subject be under the complete control of the operator for long periods of time. Not at all suitable for our purposes."

"Is this just a test run, then?" Napoleon hazarded.

"Yes, our first field application. Previously, we tested one of our own agents, not having any U.N.C.L.E. agents to practice on. Also, your men are so frequently conditioned against drugs. Terry was expendable, so we turned him into an U.N.C.L.E. admirer. Worked very well; in fact a little too well. We hadn't counted on his escape; I had a few bad moments when I realized he was on the threshold of U.N.C.L.E. headquarters with traces of the drug still in his bloodstream. Fortunately, we got him back."

"And changed him back to a loyal Thrush, I assume?"

"Oh, no. Effects are cumulative; after a certain number of doses, the conditioning is permanent. We're very close to that point here at Midford now. Once we got Terry back and completed our tests, we had to dispose of him."

"I suppose the next thing is a full scale assault on the scientists of the world?"

"We haven't decided. Probably we will seek to influence scientists, but there is always the possibility that we'll go into mass production of the drug, infiltrate the major TV networks for our messages and condition a majority of the citizenry. How does 'Whateley For President' strike you?"

Napoleon shivered inwardly but kept an outward calm. "How it would strike Thrush Central might be more to the point. They just might have other candidates in mind."

Whateley chuckled. "Yes, I suppose they might. But I control the drug, and I do think I might conjure up a few helpers from somewhere, if necessary. It wouldn't be too hard."

Napoleon shuddered slightly. "What about me? You mentioned some time ago that it was expedient for you to keep me alive."

"I'm glad you remembered the word I used, Mr. Solo. Expedient. That applies equally to Mr. Kuryakin when he arrives. As soon as I get a new batch of the drug made, you will be given massive doses, after which you will report to Mr. Waverly that the anti-U.N.C.L.E. feeling was a mere misunderstanding that has now been cleared up. And then . . . well, I'm afraid that even though I enjoy such an interesting conversationalist and splendid audience, you and Mr. Kuryakin will both have a regrettable but fatal accident on your way back to New York. It will be a pity for U.N.C.L.E. to lose their two best agents and their remarkable new car in one fell swoop, so to speak, but turnpike driving can be terribly hazardous these days."

With a final chuckle, Whateley turned and walked away down the corridor. Napoleon listened to his dying footsteps. They produced a slight echo, as though one of his demons was pattering along in front of him.

Chapter 14

"This Isn't Exactly What I Had In Mind"

AFTER RECEIVING NAPOLEON'S second call, Illya reluctantly got out of bed and dressed, meanwhile considering ways and means of getting from Lem Thompson's farm to the Whateley mansion. Lem's car had the clutch burned out, a circumstance Illya had not discovered until Lem left for Fort Wayne in his pickup truck. As a result, the only self-propelled vehicles on the farm were a tractor and a power lawn mower, neither of which seemed quite practical for driving several miles and sneaking up quietly on the Whateley house.

Once dressed, Illya picked up his communicator from the table by the bed and called the New York office. Waverly replied. Waverly always replied, no matter what time of day or night an agent called in. When he slept, or if he slept, nobody knew. Illya had heard idle speculation that the head of Section Two of U.N.C.L.E. was actually a robot. Impossible, of course, but still— when *did* the man sleep?

Illya passed along Napoleon's report on the Thrush base and inquired if any other agents were nearby and available.

"I'm afraid not, Mr. Kuryakin. The Fort Wayne agent was called to help with a case in Cleveland; we haven't had a report from the part-time agent at Midford University for some time. I'm afraid we must assume that Thrush's drug has caused a temporary, ah, shall we say defection? I will alert the Chicago office to stand by if you wish, but even with their helicopter, they are hours away. I fear that, as usual, affairs are entirely in the capable hands of Mr. Solo and yourself."

"Very well, sir. We'll do our best to handle it."

"Quite, Mr. Kuryakin. Keep me informed."

Illya stared momentarily at the silent communicator, then hurried downstairs. A minute later he was dialing Sascha Curtis' number.

In answer came the impolite noise that telephone companies use for a busy signal. Illya held the receiver out and glared at it. What was Curtis doing, using the phone at this time of night? Honest citizens should be in bed. He hesitated, but there was now little choice. U.N.C.L.E. had only one other trustworthy ally in town. Reluctantly, he called Rita Berman.

She answered almost instantly, sounding sleepy. "Who is it?"

"Illya. I'm afraid I have a favor to ask."

She yawned slightly before answering. "Ask away."

"I'm at Lem's. I have to get to Whateley's right away to help Napoleon, and I need a car. If you could pick me up here, I could drop you off at home on my way through town."

"You can have the car—on one condition."

"What's that?" Illya asked, with a sinking feeling that he already knew.

"I come with it."

"No," he said firmly. "This could be dangerous. Whateley is a Thrush, and he has quite an army at his command."

"Then," Rita pointed out, "you need all the help you can get."

"Spying on Thrush is dangerous enough for professional agents, trained for the job. It's nothing for amateurs to get mixed up in."

"Then you can't have the car. It isn't trained either, and what sort of driver would I be if I ordered my car to go where I wouldn't go myself?"

"Look, this is serious!"

"So am I. Where the car goes, I go."

Illya continued to protest, but eventually gave in. Rita promised to pick him up as soon as she could get there. She arrived a short time later. As Illya approached the car and started to enter, he came to a sudden stop.

"Professor Curtis! What are you doing here?"

"I thought you were in a hurry," Rita said. "Get in and let's go."

Illya climbed into the front seat.

"Where do you want to go?" Rita inquired. "I know you said Whateley's, but were you planning to drive up to the front door, or were you planning to try coming up on them from downwind, so to speak?"

Illya sighed resignedly. "All things considered, the more indirect the better. Is there a place where you could hide the car, say a half-mile from Whateley's house?"

"Aye, aye," she said, saluting with her free hand as she drove. Illya looked at her curiously. For the occasion, she had donned dark slacks, a sweater, a black scarf to cover her blonde hair, and a jacket with a suspicious bulge in one pocket.

"What's that?" Illya inquired, looking at the bulge. For answer, she drew out a .25 caliber Walther automatic pistol. Illya looked pained.

"That's what I was afraid it might be. Did I ever tell you that I once saw a man who had been shot seven times with one of those things?"

Rita looked horrified. "No! What happened to him?"

"He was on trial for manslaughter. After being hit seven times, he'd beaten the other fellow's head in with a shovel. If you ever have to use that, you might as well throw it at somebody. Don't bother to shoot it." He snorted. "I said this game wasn't for amateurs."

Leaving Rita looking crestfallen but determined, he swung around to Curtis. "What are you doing here?"

"I had to go right by his house," Rita explained, "and I saw his lights on, so ..."

"I've been up half the night," Curtis said. "It's this survey. All the anti-U.N.C.L.E. types have taken to calling me up in the middle of the night. It's really a very interesting phenomenon, considering the fact that the basic motivation is artificially induced. But it does get monotonous. When Rita stopped, I jumped at the chance to come. I suppose you could call it a field trip. I've never had a chance to observe actual criminals in action before. These should be particularly interesting; I've never heard of anything quite like what they are attempting in Midford. It should be fascinating; I hope to get much of it recorded." Curtis reached in one of his pockets and pulled out a miniature tape recorder.

Illya stared at the machine for a moment, then turned

to face forward and slumped down in the seat. After a few minutes of silence, Rita suddenly swung the car off the rough back road she had been traveling and rocked to a stop next to a wild raspberry thicket.

"We're well hidden," Illya admitted. "But where are we?"

"A half mile from the Whateley manse, as requested," Rita said. Illya noted unhappily that she seemed to have regained her spirit of adventure.

Curtis, meanwhile, was staring happily out the window at the raspberry patch. "I must remember this location," he said. "Raspberry yoghurt has always been one of my favorites, but it's difficult to find really good raspberries." He glanced at Illya who was beginning to look ill. "I must be sure to return here next summer."

"Now look here!" Illya shouted as he jumped out of the car. "I don't think either one of you realize what's going on. Your friend Whateley is a killer. Napoleon has found the lab where the drug is made, and it's in Whateley's basement—or in a secret passage next to the basement. Whateley is a Thrush, and regardless of what you think about him, he is not just a harmless crackpot!"

For the first time, Curtis and Rita both looked slightly taken aback.

Illya looked at both of them for a moment. "Now that I have your attention, there is something you can do if you really want to help." Rita and Sascha both nodded, somewhat submissively. "Good. First, get this car turned around so you can get out of here fast. Then get inside, lock the doors, and be ready to move quickly. If neither Napoleon nor myself gets back here within two hours, go back home and telephone this number in New York City." Illya hastily scribbled a number on a piece of paper and handed it to Curtis. "Ask for Mr. Waverly and say you have information about Solo and Kuryakin. Then tell Mr. Waverly everything, and follow his instructions. And if anyone—and I mean *anyone*—other than Napoleon or myself shows up, get going. The way things are in Midford at the moment, any of your friends could be either Thrush agents or brainwashed. Understand?"

"Perfectly, Mr. Kuryakin," came a deep voice from the darkness a few yards behind Illya. "You express yourself very well. If you will hold perfectly still and not twitch a muscle for the next few minutes, I'll allow you to go on expressing yourself, at least for awhile."

Illya did as instructed, putting a dejected slump into his back and reflecting that the sort of man who enjoyed the sound of his own voice as much as this one did would be more apt to make a mistake than a less flamboyant villain.

"All right, Mr. Kuryakin," the Thrush's voice came again. "Turn around now, slowly, with your hands behind your head. And walk just a few feet away from the car."

Illya turned to face in the same direction as Rita and Curtis. Three men stood about ten feet away. The one in the center was pointing a double-barrelled shotgun at Illya's midsection. The others had standard Thrush rifles. Behind them, a section of a hollow tree had opened like a door, revealing a stairway leading into the ground.

Illya decided it was a good thing he had suppressed his initial impulse toward immediate action. The time to fight was when your enemy was unprepared. After a moment, one of the Thrushes put down his rifle, walked behind Illya and very carefully removed his gun. Then, more boldly, he took the U.N.C.L.E. communicator and began removing various pieces of odd-looking equipment from unlikely parts of Illya's person. He paused a second.

"Are you sure this guy's an U.N.C.L.E. agent, boss? He's got enough burglar tools on him to outfit half of San Quentin."

"You search and let me do the thinking," admonished the man holding the shotgun. The searcher obediently resumed his rummaging through Illya's clothing, while Rita looked on admiringly.

"And people make jokes about women's handbags!" she exclaimed.

"No conversation," the chief Thrush snapped. "By the way, what's that bulge in your pocket? No, don't show me! Keep your hands where they are! Walker, are you through with Kuryakin yet? Get that thing out of her pocket."

The Walther was duly confiscated, as was Curtis' tape recorder, the latter over strenuous objections by the psychologist.

"But it's important that I record this!" he protested. "Think of the psychological insights that will go to waste here if I can't get this all down on tape where I can study it! What will I do for my next scientific paper?"

The Thrush chief turned to Illya. "Haven't you taught this guy the facts of life yet?" he asked in amazement.

Illya shrugged. "I tried."

The three of them were prodded into the hollow tree by the muzzles of the Thrush weapons. With the guns within reach, Illya calculated his chances of jumping his captors, but decided they were poor. He led the way down a steep stairway to an underground passage with a dirt floor and walls made of rough stone. They walked for a long way. Once or twice Illya attempted to start a casual conversation in the hope of gaining some information, but the Thrush leader discouraged conversation. Curtis, usually ready to talk under any conditions, seemed discouraged by the loss of his tape recorder; he walked along dejectedly.

They came to an intersecting passage, and the walls and floor changed to concrete. They passed two closed doors. Illya asked about them, but the Thrush leader evidently felt that he'd used up all his good lines and had no intention of talking again until he'd prepared some more. They turned down an intersecting passage. It was totally dark, with a glare of light coming from a room at the end, but before Illya could take advantage of the situation one of the guards flipped a switch and the passage was bathed in the harsh glare of naked electric bulbs. At the end of the passage was the dungeon. As they entered, Napoleon greeted them from his cell.

"When I asked you to come over and join me, this wasn't exactly what I had in mind."

"I can't say your choice of meeting places overwhelms me, either," Illya returned as he was shoved into a cell on the opposite side of the dungeon from Napoleon. Rita and Curtis were unceremoniously shoved into cells on either side of Illya.

"You'll never get away with this!" Rita called after the Thrushes as they departed.

When the Thrushes were out of earshot, Napoleon called to the others. "The place is bugged," he informed them. "That thing in the ceiling is a microphone. Whateley may or may not be listening, but don't tell me anything you wouldn't want him to hear."

Illya and Rita nodded. Professor Curtis sat grieving for his lost tape recorder.

Sounding as casual as was possible under the circumstances, Napoleon remarked, "Since they just dumped you in the cell, I assume you've been thoroughly searched?"

Illya nodded, mentally pricking his ears. Napoleon was apparently hinting that, taped and handcuffed as he was, he hadn't been totally defanged. So if any of the others could get to him . . . But most of the tools would be for escape, and if any of the others reached Napoleon, it would be because they had already escaped. Still, it was a point to remember.

Before he could think of a solution, however, there

was a commotion in the corridor. Lem Thompson appeared, wrestled along with a Thrush holding each arm and a third prodding him with a Thrush rifle.

Chapter 15

"Clumsiness Pays Off Again"

LEM WAS GIVING HIS captors as much trouble as he could without getting violent enough to provoke them into shooting him. After considerable profanity on both sides, he was shoved roughly into a cell. As the Thrushes departed down the corridor, he shook his fist after them.

"You'll pay for this!" he yelled.

Napoleon cocked an eyebrow at Illya. "What do you bet the next prisoner says 'You can't do this to me!'?"

"I don't think there's anyone left to be taken prisoner," Illya observed. "How did they get you, Lem? I thought you were . . ."

"I was!" Lem returned. "That'll teach me to mind my own business. After this, you guys run your own errands. And either you or them Thrush characters better pay for my truck, too!"

"I think our insurance covers it," Napoleon said. "But what happened?"

"What didn't!" Lem said indignantly. "I just got out on the road and this car comes roarin' along, tries to run me into the ditch. Well, two can play at that, and my pickup's bigger'n their car. So when they cut in front of me, I rammed 'em. They ended up halfway across the field, but I spun into the ditch, too, and then this other car came up and swarmed all over me." Lem lost his indignation for a moment and chuckled slightly at a recollection.

"They were runnin' around like chickens with their

heads chopped off. Couple of 'em hung onto me and the rest drug their buddies outa the other car. Pretty banged up, too. Finally one of 'em dug out this little thing and jabbered into it. Musta been someone on the other end, cause it chattered right back at him. Ended up takin' me to the old Ryan place, just across from my farm, and took the banged up ones somewhere to get patched up. Guess they been usin' Ryan's place—he's away somewheres—to spy on me. Or on you two!" he concluded accusingly.

"What about the drug?" Napoleon asked.

"One of 'em said it got spilled in the wreck. They was gonna put somethin' else in its place and send it to that Waverly fella. Guess they did. Finally they got me and carted me over here."

"We seem to be damaging their transportation at least," Napoleon observed. "But I don't think that will slow down their major plans very much."

"Quite a good summation, Mr. Solo," came a distinctive voice from the corridor. Jabez Whateley strolled into the dungeon area. He appeared in fine humor as he leaned on a corner of the rack and beamed—as much as anyone with his countenance could beam—at the prisoners.

"Actually," he continued, "you and Mr. Kuryakin did the most effective damage when you destroyed the stocks of the drug at Bippus. I'm afraid that was my own fault, though. *The Purloined Letter* was always one of my favorite stories, but I shouldn't have allowed it to affect my judgment. Of course, I hadn't counted on your moving so rapidly; I'm afraid I underestimated you a trifle."

"Yes," Napoleon agreed. "It was a little careless, leaving the entire supply of the drug in plain sight that way."

Whateley shrugged. "It won't take long to brew a new batch. Tomorrow evening at the latest, and we shouldn't be disturbed before then. After all, when the drug sample Waverly receives proves to be a harmless coloring additive—well, what would you think in his place? Then the two of you will call in and report your mistakes in person. Your last reports, I fear," he concluded sadly.

"Don't get all broken up about it," Napoleon said sympathetically. "It's all part of the job, and all that."

"True," Whateley agreed. "Quite true. I do hope you won't take it personally. I do regret it; you're such a good listener."

"What about the others?" Napoleon asked. "They haven't done you any harm, and they aren't members of U.N.C.L.E., so . . ."

Whateley shook his head. "I suppose we could eventually convert them, but it would be very inconvenient, and there is always the chance that in a long project like that, someone would get careless. Not to mention that we shall have to remain on constant alert in case U.N.-C.L.E. does send in more agents before we have completed our test here. No, I'm afraid there's nothing for it but to eliminate them."

Whateley stood looking mournful for a few moments, then consulted his watch and brightened. "Time for phase two," he said cheerfully. "I must be on hand for all stages of drug preparation. I'll keep you informed of my progress; it's the least I can do as a host." He switched off all the lights except the one in the dungeon and walked off down the dark corridor.

Curtis had recovered his interest and now looked thoughtful. "The man's mind is definitely unbalanced. Perhaps the next time he comes down here to gloat, I can apply my psychological insight. Manipulating him would be difficult, of course; one never knows precisely how an unstable mind will react."

"Be my guest," said Napoleon. "Any reaction other than killing us outright will be welcome. In the meantime, however, we need to work on more direct means of escape."

Silence fell as the prisoners pondered their situation. Napoleon worked steadily in an attempt to get the tape off his fingers.

Whateley had been gone for some time when there was a slight noise from the corridor. The prisoners looked up to see Flavia Whateley entering the dungeon. Rita began to smile hopefully.

"What's a nice girl like you doing in a place like this?" Napoleon inquired.

"Getting you out of here, I hope," she replied. She was now fully in the light, and they could see she had a welding hood pushed back on her head and was pulling a small rubber-tired cart loaded with acetylene and oxygen tanks, hose, gauges, and a cutting torch.

"I knew we could count on you," Rita exclaimed.

Flavia smiled faintly. "I expected you to think I was a devil-worshipper and a Thrush, like Father. I hadn't realized—I thought all of his talk about gods and demons was just a pose. Oh, I knew that Grandfather had really believed himself to be a wizard, but Father had been educated; he was really a brilliant man. I just don't know what happened to him."

"What's likely to happen to us is more important right now," Rita said. "Get that torch going, kid."

"How did you find us?" Napoleon asked as she lit the torch. "Your father said you didn't know anything about these passages."

"I didn't," she said, starting to work on the bars of Rita's cell. "I was in an old storage room in the basement a while ago when I heard a noise outside one of the walls. As far as I knew there weren't any passages there, so I went over and investigated. There had been some junk piled against that wall—I was looking through it for some copper tubing that was put down here somewhere—but I'd moved most of it. Once I had the rest out of the way it wasn't hard to find the door."

"Clumsiness pays off again," Napoleon commented. "That noise was me."

"Anyway," Flavia continued, "I overheard Father when he was talking to you; when he said he'd have to eliminate everybody. In fact, when he started to leave, I barely got out of the passage ahead of him. Then I followed him back to his study, and listened. He was starting an incantation! I could hear him muttering, deciding what demon to summon, and for the first time I knew he wasn't joking."

"Did he get any results?" Illya inquired.

"He didn't finish it. I think he must have been missing an ingredient. He cursed a lot, and I could hear him open drawers and things, looking for something. Then he came out and got in his car and drove away and I came down here. I suppose he's gone to buy something."

"I wonder what ingredient for a spell one could purchase at a corner drugstore?" Illya mused. By now Rita was free and Flavia wheeled her cart over to Napoleon's cell. In a few minutes, all the prisoners were free.

"The next problem," said Illya, "is to get to the car."

"How do we get there?" Napoleon inquired. "I assume it was put in the garage to avoid curious eyes, but how do we reach the garage from here?"

"If you don't want to go tramping back through Whateley's study," Illya suggested, "how about the passage they brought us in through? It had some branching corridors."

"It's worth a try." Napoleon turned to Flavia. "Do you have any idea where we are in relation to the house and grounds?"

She stood quietly for a minute, mentally retracing her steps through the passages. "We should be about in the middle of the back yard," she said finally. "The garage will be back this way." She led the way through the corridors, turning now and then when she came to an intersection. Eventually they encountered a short stairway. Napoleon led the way up. After a short period of experimenting, he pushed open the door at the top of the stairway and the group stepped out into a grease pit, one wall of which was the door. There was a car parked over the pit but it left enough space for them to climb out.

The garage was large but crowded. Besides the U.N.-C.L.E. car, there were two damaged Thrush vehicles plus Lem Thompson's pickup truck. A third wrecked car, which Napoleon recognized as the hotrod which had plowed into the Beaver Dam Muck Festival, sat outside an open door, next to a wrecker made of a twelve-cylinder Packard roadster with the rumble seat removed and a hoist installed. The damaged cars had been partially dismantled; evidently some Thrush mechanic had been working on them. Luckily, the U.N.C.L.E. car had not been locked, and Illya hurriedly entered and opened the weapons compartment. He looked unhappy as he pulled out the Mercox and a handful of projectiles.

"We're short of ammunition for this," he said. "One tear gas, half a dozen high explosive, and three hypodermic darts."

"But aren't you going to get away?" Flavia said.

"Our job is to stop this entire business," Napoleon explained. "But it might be a good idea for you to leave before the shooting starts. You could take the wrecker out there."

"Not on your life!" Rita objected. "You're not going to catch me running around in one of Thrush's pet cars when Thrush agents could be anywhere in town. At least if I stay here I'll have some protection."

"If we could make it to my place you'd have protection," Lem said.

"Sure, if. I know you have a regular arsenal out there,

but I've got no assurance that Thrush would let us get that far."

"I agree with Rita," Curtis said. "In addition, I would hesitate to miss this unique opportunity to study a criminal organization in its native habitat."

"You got queer ideas of fun," Lem grumbled, but he made no move toward the Packard.

Napoleon nodded. "Much as I hate to say it, Rita does have a good argument. It might be safer to stick together."

"But what are you going to do?" demanded Flavia.

"Stop your father, somehow," Napoleon replied.

"But you can't just shoot him down!"

"That's what he was goin' to do to us," Lem reminded her.

"But he's sick! He needs a psychiatrist, not a firing squad!"

"Don't worry," Illya answered her. "It's U.N.C.L.E.'s policy to avoid killing except as a last resort. The more help you can give us, the less likely we are to have to resort to violence to capture him. This," he held up the Mercox, "is an ideal weapon for the purpose, if we can get in position to use it." He explained.

Flavia was still reluctant, but eventually agreed to aid them. Meanwhile, Napoleon had been digging through the weapons compartment; now he backed out of the U.N.C.L.E. car with an armload of weapons. He kept an U.N.C.L.E. Special for himself and gave one to Lem, handed a riot shotgun to Professor Curtis and a revolver loaded with tear gas cartridges to Rita. Illya carried the Mercox.

"What now?" Rita asked.

"Since our prime object is to capture Jabez Whateley," Napoleon said, "and since Illya has the only weapon we can use for that, we'll have to stick together. All we could accomplish by splitting up would be for one of us to run into a Thrush and give advance warning that we'd escaped."

"While we're waiting for Whateley to come back, we might do some damage to his lab," Illya suggested.

"No, if we capture Whateley, the lab is automatically rendered useless, since he is the only Thrush who knows how to manufacture the drug. Similarly, destroying the existing supplies won't help much if Whateley escapes to start over again somewhere else." Napoleon thought a moment. "We'd better contact Mr. Waverly. He can get reinforcements sent in from Chicago; the more men we have, the easier it will be to make a capture without having to kill anybody." He turned to Flavia. "Do you have any idea where your father put our communicators?"

Flavia shook her head. "Maybe in his study, but I don't know."

"All right, the study it is. If we can't find the communicators, we can use the car's computer to transmit the message. The trouble is that it will transmit it to the New York data banks and not to Mr. Waverly personally and we can't tell when the message will reach him. But we can try as a last resort."

"There's a signal transmitter with printed readout in the car," Illya said.

"Not now there isn't. I tried that when I was getting the weapons. Thrush has been at it. I suppose we might be able to repair it, but finding the communicators would be easier."

Napoleon led the way to Whateley's study, where Lem was posted to watch the hall and Professor Curtis to watch the secret entrances while the rest of the group searched. There were no communicators. Illya found a file of Thrush records and extracted a few of the more valuable papers, but there was nothing in the room which would aid them in capturing Jabez Whateley.

Finally Napoleon gave up the search. "They aren't here. We'll go back to the car. I'll try the computer link while Illya sees if he can repair the transmitter. Be careful; there may still be some Thrushes around and we don't want to give Whateley advance warning that we're loose."

After a cautious look around, they slipped out into the back yard and headed for the garage. They were halfway there when they heard the crunch of tires on gravel and a pair of brilliant headlights swept around the corner of the house and fell directly on them.

Chapter 16

"It's A Little Late To Call Mr. Waverly"

"THE GARAGE!" NAPOLEON SHOUTED as he lunged forward. "The car's our best chance."

The driver apparently anticipated their destination, for the engine roared and the tires spun as it raced for the garage itself. The sound of a gun came from somewhere behind the headlights and Napoleon heard something thunk into the ground just ahead of him.

He skidded to a halt as he realized they were cut off. "Back to the house!" he shouted and started for the back door himself, herding the others in front of him.

Before they had covered half the distance, the back door started to open. Illya, now in the lead, fired the only thing he had, the Mercox with a tear gas load. It crashed into the wall next to the door and burst into a cloud of white. The door slammed shut on a cough.

Casting about desperately, Illya detoured to the right toward the only available cover he could see: a rickety

147

fence and an area of rank grass, bushes, a few old trees, and what might, except for their regular shapes, have been occasional boulders peering through the grass. Napoleon followed Illya's lead and herded the others ahead of him toward the fence.

Another shot sounded from behind him and Napoleon loosed some hasty shots over his shoulder as he ran.

They were at the fence now. Illya vaulted it easily, then reached back to yank Rita over bodily. At the same time, Sascha and Lem clambered over, a bit less athletically; Napoleon boosted Flavia and hurriedly dived over himself. There was another flurry of shots from the vicinity of the garage, and a slight groan from somewhere ahead of Napoleon, followed by some colorful cursing.

In another second, they were all out of sight in the grass, behind either trees or stones. What had looked like boulders in the dim light now turned out to be tombstones. Napoleon found himself sharing an extra large stone with Lem Thompson, who was clutching his right shoulder and muttering to himself. Before Napoleon could say anything, Lem glared at him accusingly.

"Nothin' busted, I don't think," Lem said. "You boys better have some damn good insurance! First my truck, and now me!"

"Here, let me—" Napoleon started to reach toward Lem's injured shoulder, but Lem batted his hand away.

"Never you mind! If you need as much help doctorin' as you do secret agentin', I'd as soon take my chances."

Napoleon got a brief glance at the wound when Lem batted at him with his left hand, and he decided that Lem was right. He'd be fine—if they could get out of here.

The shooting from the garage had stopped when they reached cover, so Napoleon risked a quick look over the top of the stone. There was no immediate fire. He looked around to locate the other members of the group. He spotted Illya behind a tree to his right; Flavia was crouching behind another tombstone a few yards to his left.

"Where are we?" he whispered loudly to Flavia.

"The Whateley cemetery," she said. "Although the only Whateleys in it are my grandparents. It was on the land when he got it, and—well, until now I thought it was just more of his and father's sense of humor, with all the wild trees and grass they planted to make it look mouldering. Grandfather's vault is over there."

Flavia gestured toward a dark stone structure twenty yards behind them. Napoleon hadn't noticed it before, since it was half-hidden among the trees and bushes. At first glance it seemed an ideal defensive position, but he quickly saw that this was deceptive. There were no windows, the door was the only exit, and once inside, the defenders would be bottled up while Thrush readied enough high explosives to blow the place down around their ears.

Napoleon crouched down and made a short dash to the tree and joined Illya.

"What do you think?" Illya asked. "Can we hold out?"

"Probably," Napoleon replied. "I don't think they have enough manpower to rush us over that open ground. But we're low on ammunition. And besides, holding out isn't enough. We have to get Whateley somehow. If he gets away, he can set up shop somewhere else. We might never find him until too late."

Illya nodded. "I don't quite see how we can stop him, though. They can't get at us, but at the same time, we can't get at them."

Napoleon suddenly smiled. "What about the vault?"

Illya glanced around in the direction Napoleon was looking. He spotted the massive structure, and the same idea occurred to him. "A secret passage, you mean? But if there is, we'd better hurry or Whateley will be popping out of it himself."

"You keep a watch on the garage and house. I'll check with Flavia." Napoleon ducked down into the grass again and scurried over to Flavia's tombstone.

Flavia frowned at the question. "Not that I know of —but, then, I didn't know about all those others, either."

"It's worth a try. Keep down in the grass and start for the vault. I'll round up the rest and join you."

Napoleon moved back to Lem first. "Think you can make it all right?"

"I made it this far, didn't I? You just worry about yourself; that oughta keep you occupied." Lem released his shoulder and peered at it for a moment. It seemed to have stopped bleeding. He moved the damaged shoulder experimentally, then got down on all fours and started back toward the vault.

Back at Illya's tree, the two agents looked out at the garage. The car's headlights were still burning but it was out of sight around the building. There was no activity evident from their vantage point.

"You round up Rita and Sascha," Napoleon said, "and I'll get back to the vault and investigate."

Illya nodded agreement. "But first I think we should give Thrush something to think about while we're inside the vault." He loaded one of the high explosive projectiles into the Mercox, aimed carefully at a garage window, and fired.

The shot missed the window and pulverized a concrete block next to it, but it was close enough to bring a chorus of excited shouts from inside the garage. Illya lobbed a second round at the building; this one went through the window and exploded inside. It produced more shouting and indications that Thrush was vacating the garage interior.

Illya stuffed the Mercox under his belt and started looking for the two errant members of the party.

By this time, Napoleon had reached the vault and found Flavia already there, at the bottom of a short flight of steps that led to the door. Lem was crouched down at the top of the steps, still holding his pistol. Napoleon hurried down the steps and helped Flavia push on the door. After a few seconds, it began to creak slowly open.

The interior of the vault was nearly barren, except for a heavy coating of dust and cobwebs. The deep recesses in the walls were empty. A single, ornate casket lay on a carved dais in the center of the floor.

"Jabez, Senior?" Napoleon inquired.

Flavia nodded, and the two of them started searching for anything that looked like it might conceal a secret door. They hadn't found anything when, a minute later, Rita and Sascha hurriedly entered the vault and Illya's voice came excitedly from outside.

"Napoleon! Get back up here! They're up to something."

"Stay put," Napoleon snapped to Flavia, "and you two help her look for the entrance to a secret passage." He ran out the door to find Illya crouched next to Lem at the head of the stairs. "You, too," he said to Lem. "The more, the merrier."

Illya had already started to move and was impatiently motioning for Napoleon to follow. As they moved back toward the front of the cemetery, the first thing Napoleon noticed was that the lights behind the garage had gone out. "They've been clanking and pounding back there ever since you left," Illya said as they reached his tree. "I can't see what they're up to, but—"

He broke off as they both saw what the clanking had been for. The Thrushes had been building a tank. Heavy steel plates had been hastily mounted on the front of one of their cars, which now rumbled around the corner of the garage and headed directly for the cemetery.

"You take the tires," Illya said, fitting one of the remaining high explosive rounds into the Mercox. "I'll see what these do." Aiming at a point where two plates joined, he fired. The explosion rocked the vehicle, but failed to stop it. Hastily he fired a second round with no more effect, and now it was within yards of the fence.

As Illya reloaded a third time, one of Napoleon's shots hit a tire, and the car swerved to one side. Seizing his only chance, Illya put the last of his high explosive rounds into the gas tank.

The results were spectacular. A huge fireball burst from the stricken car and roared upward. Two Thrushes leaped out, their clothing on fire, and rolled on the grass in front of the fence. The car was still burning fiercely as the fire in their clothing was extinguished. They entered the cemetery meekly when Napoleon ordered them to do so.

Shielded from any Thrushes remaining in the garage by the flaming car, the two agents herded the Thrushes back to the vault. They were almost there when a series of explosions came from behind them. Napoleon kept his gun trained on the Thrushes, but Illya glanced back to see what had happened.

"The car," he said. "That's why they wanted to get close to us. They had more explosives in there."

Napoleon prodded the two scorched Thrushes into the vault and sat them down back to back in one corner. Then he took their belts and tied their hands together behind their backs.

This accomplished, he rejoined Illya at the top of the stairs. The car, now scattered in pieces over several square yards, had stopped burning.

"What's next, I wonder?" Illya looked toward the garage and house.

"After that homemade tank trick, I begin to suspect that Whateley is back from the drug store. They were pretty disorganized at first or they might have picked us all off at the start. But now somebody is directing things. I know what I'd do in Whateley's place, and I suspect the only thing holding him back is your Mercox. Do you have any more high explosive rounds?"

Illya shook his head.

"That's what I was afraid of. If Whateley suspects as much, we may be in for a hot time."

For the time being, Thrush activity seemed to have ceased. An occasional shot came from one of the windows in the house, but whoever was shooting could hardly hope to see his target. The firing seemed to be either simple harassment or an attempt to draw a return.

Then the sound Napoleon had been dreading came. There was the distinctive roar of an auto engine; a moment later, the U.N.C.L.E. car rounded the corner of the garage. They couldn't see the driver, but both Illya and Napoleon knew it had to be Jabez Whateley. The man wouldn't trust any of his subordinates to handle the vehicle.

He was driving slowly, evidently enjoying the moment and determined to prolong it as much as possible. Slowly a section of the grille retracted and the snouts of the flame throwers slid into view. There was an almost invisible flash from the laser system, and a neat round hole appeared in the vault a yard above their heads.

Napoleon could picture Whateley chuckling to himself as he tested the weapons.

Illya glanced at the Mercox, useless now without the high explosives. "I might as well get something useful," he muttered and ran back down the steps. A second later he was back with Sascha's riotgun and Lem's pistol.

In the meantime, Napoleon had attached the shoulder stock and telescopic sight to the U.N.C.L.E. Special, converting it into a carbine. "If he's going to use the rockets, he'll have to raise the door. Maybe . . ." The laser flickered again, and a second hole appeared, lower down this time. Napoleon glanced up. "But I don't think we can wait." He sighted carefully and began firing. Illya followed suit, first with the riot shotgun, then with the pistol. The car body was plastic, strong but not impregnable. With high explosives, it could have been stopped, but the chances were slim with conventional ammunition. But they had to try.

They were both firing and reloading as rapidly as they could, but the sweeping contours of the car presented no surface for a solid hit. The bullets struck glancing blows and whined off into the distance. The bullet-proof glass in the windshield protected Whateley completely.

The car crept closer. Then the door opened, just a crack. Napoleon quickly sighted and fired. The bullet ricocheted off harmlessly and before he could fire a second time, there was a *woosh* of fire. Both agents dived back down the steps and flattened themselves at the bottom. A moment later, about a yard from where they had been at the top of the steps, an explosion rocked the vault.

The two agents had been protected by the steps, but next time . . . "How many of those does he have?" Napoleon asked.

"Enough to get our range," Illya said. "At least half a dozen. We're just lucky that the heat seeking system isn't sensitive enough to respond to body heat."

At that instant, Rita and Sascha came bursting through the vault door. Each had an U.N.C.L.E. Special.

Napoleon stared at them unbelievingly for a second. "Where did you get those?" he snapped.

"We couldn't find a passage," Rita said. "But there was a little compartment in the coffin. And it's more useful than that tear gas gun, so—"

Napoleon wasn't waiting for the complete story. He leaped up and dashed inside the vault. "Everyone inside!" he shouted as he disappeared through the door.

Puzzled, Illya and the others followed. "Shove the door shut!" Napoleon said over his shoulder as he moved around the dais until he found the coffin's compartment and began rummaging furiously.

As he pulled something out, another rocket hit the vault; the entire structure shook. One of the empty recesses crumbled and dust flew in the door, which Illya and Curtis were trying to force shut.

Illya glanced back and saw that Napoleon had an U.N.C.L.E. communicator in his hand. "It's a little late to call Mr. Waverly," he said.

But Napoleon was making quick adjustments on the communicator, then speaking into it rapidly.

Suddenly, there was silence. The deep throated rumble of the U.N.C.L.E. car's engine was gone.

Napoleon pocketed the communicator and breathed a huge sigh of relief, and started toward the vault door. "Let's go take possession of the car and Whateley. I don't think we'll have any trouble from the rest of the Thrushes once we've done that."

Comprehension suddenly came to Illya. "The anti-theft program in the computer . . ."

"Exactly," Napoleon said. "When it receives the code I just sent, it shuts off all power, locks the brakes, and looses a fast-acting anesthetic gas into the driver's compartment."

The two agents hurried out to the car. In the east, the first light of dawn was beginning to show.

Professor Curtis produced a quart jar from his refrigerator and held it up proudly. "Midford, '59," he explained. "A very good year for rose hip extract."

Lem Thompson looked decidedly uneasy until Curtis

pulled several glasses from a cabinet and began filling them from the jar. "Oh, it's for drinking," he said, relief showing in his voice. "Looked like more medicine, there for a minute. I got enough of that for a month of Sundays." He glanced at his arm, swathed in bandages and supported in a sling.

Napoleon, even though he had tasted Curtis' concoctions before, managed a polite smile as Curtis handed him a glass. Illya merely looked glum. Rita Berman thought of her grades and put on a cheerful face.

"Did you and that little man in your fountain pen get everything worked out last night?" Rita asked as she sipped cautiously.

Napoleon ignored Illya's startled glance as he replied. "Yes, everything's under control. Mr. Waverly got some men from the Chicago branch to take the Thrushes off our hands. They're probably in New York by now."

"Jabez, too?" she wanted to know. "In spite of everything—well, I just can't believe he would have followed through on his threats."

"Hah!" Lem said, touching his bandaged arm. "I suppose this ain't following through enough for you?"

"I'm afraid Lem is right," Napoleon said, "but we have hopes for Jabez. U.N.C.L.E. has some pretty good men on its psychiatric staff, you know."

"In other words," Lem snorted, "you're gonna do to him what he was gonna do to us."

"You can't say that curing an unbalanced mind is the same as drugging an entire community!" Rita exclaimed.

"All depends on who's in charge of the balance, I guess," Lem said philosophically. "Besides, I didn't say I was against it. Letting him off too easy, if you ask me. None of my business, though. Just so I get my truck fixed, and get all the farm work done." He looked meaningfully at his injured arm.

"It's all been taken care of," Napoleon assured him. "Mr. Waverly said he'd have a check in the mail for you today. And one of the Chicago agents will be down to help you out until your arm is better."

"What about Flavia?" Rita asked. "I haven't seen her since last night."

"She s coming back to New York," Napoleon said. "She decided that a sink-or-swim effort at her sculpting would be the best thing for her."

"You aren't planning on giving her a lift, are you?" Illya asked, a note of incipient claustrophobia in his voice.

Napoleon considered for a moment. "You must admit, it wouldn't be quite the same as it was with Dr. Armden," he said, then hurried on as he noted Illya's dour look. "No, she's coming later. It will be a few days before she can close up the mansion. And then she has to get her tools and all the rest shipped ahead."

Before Rita had a chance to comment, Napoleon's communicator sounded.

"Solo here."

"Ah, yes, Mr. Solo," came Waverly's voice. "I've been in contact with Whateley, through the agents bringing him in. He mentioned some rather unusual volumes in his library. I was hoping that, before you left—"

"Considering the nature of his, ah, delusions," Napoleon interrupted "do you think it wise to let him have access to his books?"

"Oh, no, Mr. Solo, not for Whateley. There are a few I would be interested in seeing myself, if you could arrange to pick them up before you leave."

"They might give you an insight into the workings of his mind," Illya offered helpfully.

"Quite right, Mr. Kuryakin; they could be invaluable to our psychiatric staff in their treatment of Whateley. Though I must admit a certain personal curiosity myself. The world of the occult and the like, you know."

"Certainly, sir," Napoleon said. "You had some particular volumes in mind?"

Illya listened as Napoleon copied down a dozen or more titles. "You don't suppose," he said dubiously, once Napoleon had signed off, "that Mr. Waverly would ever *really* try to dispatch agents by broomstick?"

If you have missed any full-length U.N.C.L.E. adventures starring Napoleon Solo and Illya Kuryakin, ask your newsdealer for them, or use order form below:

DON'T MISS THESE GREAT ADVENTURES
IN TIME-TRAVEL INTRIGUE!